O Little Town

O LITTLE TOWN

A NOVEL

DON REID

David C Cook

transforming lives together

O LITTLE TOWN
Published by David C. Cook
4050 Lee Vance View
Colorado Springs, CO 80918 U.S.A.

David C. Cook Distribution Canada
55 Woodslee Avenue, Paris, Ontario, Canada N3L 3E5

David C. Cook U.K., Kingsway Communications
Eastbourne, East Sussex BN23 6NT, England

David C. Cook and the graphic circle C logo
are registered trademarks of Cook Communications Ministries.

This story is a work of fiction. All characters and events are
the product of the author's imagination. Any resemblance
to any person, living or dead, is coincidental.

LCCN 2008931897
ISBN 978-1-4347-9930-2

© 2008 Don Reid
Published in association with The Seymour Agency,
475 Miner Street Road, Canton, NY 13617

The Team: Don Pape, Steve Parolini, Amy Kiechlin,
Jaci Schneider, and Susan Vannaman
Cover Design: GearBox, David Carlson
Cover Photo: © Getty Images, Alan Thornton
Interior Design: Boswell Idea Group

Printed in Canada
First Edition 2008

1 2 3 4 5 6 7 8 9 10

071508

For my best friend,
Bobby,
and all the Christmas Eves before

ACKNOWLEDGMENTS

Let me start by thanking the people at David C. Cook, who saw enough merit in these pages to want to publish them. Then I'd like to thank my agent, Mary Sue Seymour, who called their attention to these pages. She's a sweet lady who jumped on this thing from day one and made it happen. Thanks also to Steve Parolini, my editor. I was sweating him the most; but he turned out to be one of the good guys. He knows his business, understands people, and is a fair man. You can't ask for more than that.

But I always seemed to get more than I deserved. My pal and attorney, Russ Farrar, put the deal together. My lovely wife, Debbie, and brother, Harold, and sons, Debo and Langdon, and writer/friend Charles Culbertson read the chapters as I wrote them and told me how wonderful they were. Sometimes they even told me the *truth*, and I went back and fixed things and made them right.

And I can't forget my hometown of Staunton, Virginia. I borrowed its streets and buildings and landmarks and houses and churches for this book. Only the name was changed. I'm not exactly sure why I did that, but I liked "Mt. Jefferson" and eventually came to love it. I hope you will too.

CHAPTER

From where I'm sitting, I can see where most of it took place. Down Main Street, clear to the end of the block, is where Macalbee's Five and Dime used to be. Then up this way, in the middle of the block, was the old police station. And if you look clear to the top of the hill, you can see the steeple from the Mason Street Methodist Church. Back then, if you listened carefully, you could hear the bell ring every morning at precisely nine o'clock—it was so dependable people opened their stores to it. And then right down there, of course, is the Crown Theater.

I don't remember the story from first-hand experience, of course, but I've heard it told often enough that it's almost as if I'd actually been there. It could have happened anywhere. In any town. In any state. But it happened in this town, Mt. Jefferson, and in a state of Christmas bustle like we haven't seen here in half a century. The sidewalks were overflowing with shoppers and the shoppers were overflowing with packages and snow was blowing and the Salvation Army ringers were ringing and people were filling their kettles. Elvis was on the radio, Ike was in the White House, and the Lord was in his holy temple. It was Christmas 1958.

Actually it was two days before Christmas. Tuesday morning. 10:15. And it all started with a knock on the door of Milton Sandridge's second-floor office, which overlooked the sales floor of Macalbee's Five and Dime.

"Mr. Sandridge. Mr. Sandridge. It's urgent, Mr. Sandridge."

"Come in, Lois." Milton stood and walked around his desk, as he could tell by his assistant manager's voice something unusual was in the air.

As she opened the door, the look on her face matched the sound of her words. "We've got a shoplifter in aisle three."

They both turned and looked through the office window that gave an eagle's-eye view of everything and everybody in the store. Milton counted seven customers in aisle three. A mother with a baby in a stroller, a lone woman with a scarf tied under her chin, a colored woman with two small boys hanging on her coattail, and one teenage girl in jeans and a pea jacket. Milton looked back at Lois, shrugged, raised his eyebrows, and turned up the palms of his hands. She read his question and answered with the precision he always expected from her.

"The girl. Ponytail and dungarees. She's stuffing her pockets."

"Is somebody on the doors?"

"Ernest is watching both front doors and Tiny is watching the back."

"Do they know not to approach her until she hits the sidewalk?"

"They won't do anything till they hear from me. Or you."

"Have them stop her on the street. Take someone with you and bring her back to the storeroom and call the cops. You know the routine."

"Ah, there's a little more to it this time, I'm afraid."

"What do you mean?"

"Apparently you didn't get a good look at her. We know who she is."

"Lois, it's two days till Christmas. The store is filling up. We've got four people out with the flu and everything I ordered from the Sears catalog this year is late. Just tell me what's up. Who is she?"

"Millie Franklin."

"That's supposed to mean something to me?"

"Rev. Paul Franklin, up at the Methodist Church. His daughter."

This was the moment the palpitations started. That stuff about Sears and four people out with influenza and the store getting fuller by the minute didn't hold a candle to this. Millie Franklin. Why hadn't that name registered the first time he heard it? The season must have dulled his senses. But whatever it was going to take to awaken those senses now was going to have to happen in the next thirty seconds. Something had to be done before Millie got to the sidewalk because once she was there, she was a criminal, and there was nothing he could do about it.

Milton and Lois looked into each other's eyes and connected for only a second, then turned and squeezed through the office door at the same time and down the back steps running.

When they hit the landing, he said, "You get the back door, and I'll get the front. Make sure she doesn't get outside. If you spot her, let me know and I'll approach her." Milton knew the responsibility was his, but there was something more than duty to the store in his urgent tone. There was something personal here but no one saw it at the time. No one *could* see it. Milton was moving too fast for anyone to get a good look at his eyes and the pallor of his skin.

Lois headed for the back of the store and Milton to the front. There, just as he was supposed to be was the janitor Ernest Tolley, dressed in his signature bib overalls, plaid shirt, tie, and dress hat. He turned his head with each customer who entered or exited the front doors like he was an angel guarding the Garden of Eden.

"Has she come this way, Ernest?" Milton asked, his feet never stopping.

"No, sir. I ain't seen her or I'd a nabbed her."

"Sit on her if you have to," Milton said as he walked hurriedly back through the store, checking each wide, wooden-floored aisle. But no Millie. And where was Lois and why wasn't she covering her half of the store? He was almost at the back door when he saw three figures through the glass, huddled on the sidewalk. Lois and Tiny Grant, the store's other janitor, stood on either side of Millie Franklin, holding her by the arms. Milton's palpitations were immediately cured as his heart stopped beating altogether.

Milton looked back to discover that three clerks, curious, frightened, and amazed, had followed him and were standing, staring, and waiting for his next move. It had already gone too far. At least six people knew what had happened. Heaven only knows how many customers had already picked up on the excitement and the whispers. It was too late to do anything except the right thing, the expected thing. He would have to bring her into the storeroom, call the police, and hold her until they questioned her, searched her, and arrested her.

Macalbee's had strict policies about how such matters were to be handled, which left little room for innovation. Any one of the onlookers could say the wrong word at the wrong time and the home office in Richmond would have wind of it before sun set on another day. That's how it was with a chain store. Oh, he might not get fired, of course, but Milton didn't want any negative attention to his managerial style.

Despite the name, Macalbee's Five and Dime was not a nickel-and-dime operation. It started as a family store in the state's capital nearly a quarter of a century earlier and had grown steadily throughout the South ever since. The Mt. Jefferson branch was the twenty-third to open, and Milton felt lucky to be part of such a flourishing company. And yet even in this most guarded of moments, standing here with all his employees seeing everything but his private thoughts, he had to admit to himself that Richmond and the revered Macalbee family was not the only reason he was dreading this present situation. The preacher's kid? Bad enough. But he was more concerned right now with the wrath of her mother.

Milton closed his eyes and rubbed his forehead and inhaled a deep breath that he wished had been full of Chesterfield tar and nicotine. But a cigarette would have to wait. He had some work to do.

CHAPTER

Buddy Briggs was a local boy who went into WWII with a young wife and came out with a young daughter he saw for the first time when she was three years old. He never wanted to leave either one of them again, and he didn't. He tempered his dream of being the best pilot in the service and instead used what he'd learned in the Army to become the best cop in a small town that needed him. With those adventures behind him, now he sat behind a desk that both hampered him and protected him from life's opportunities and disappointments.

Lt. Briggs was on the phone in the small cubbyhole his subordinates called his office. One of two plain-clothesmen on the force, today he felt the full weight of his enviable position. That wasn't a lawyer or a witness on the other end of the phone. It wasn't the mechanic up the street telling him his car was ready or the dress shop on the corner calling to say his order was finally in. It was his wife, Amanda, and the news she just shared caused his face to turn from red to white and back to red again.

On the second cycle of changing colors, a sergeant poked his head in the door and handed him a note. Buddy glanced at it and laid it on the desk ink blotter.

"Amanda, I've gotta go. No, it's not more important than what you're telling me, but it's my job. I gotta go. I'll call you back just as soon as I can. I do care, and I'll take care of it. We'll take care of it. I promise you. Okay. Okay. Good-bye."

But then he just sat there, pulled from the conversation not by the urgency in the note—though it was important to him—but by the urgency to have a minute to himself to consider what his wife had just told him. He needed to cool down and use all his professional power to stay calm and reasonable. He looked back at the note, frowned and yelled for the sergeant.

"Carl. What's this all about? A shoplifter at Macalbee's and you're giving it to me? Don't I have a few more important things to do around here than question a shop-lifter in a dime store?"

"Your pal from the store called. What's his name?"

"Milton?"

"Yeah, Sandridge. Milton Sandridge. He said to give it to you and to nobody else. He wants you to come personally."

"That's all you got?"

"I just take the messages, Lieutenant. You want me to send Sikes or Trainum?"

"No, I'll take care of it." At this he picked up the phone again and dialed the number from memory. Lois, always the efficient assistant manager, answered on the first ring. He could almost see her small, prim face under her tight, prim permanent and could even hear the per-petual worry lines around her tired gray eyes in the way she said, "Macalbee's. Merry Christmas."

"Lois, let me talk to Milton."

"He's not here. He's down in the storeroom. You want me to go get him?"

Feeling the weight of all of his forty-two Christmases coming down on his shoulders, he sighed and said, "No," and put the phone back in its cradle. He put on his over-coat and hat and walked out the door and down the alley for a half a block and into the back door of Macalbee's. He knocked before opening the storeroom door and found Milton Sandridge sitting on a box of draperies, smoking.

Milton's receding hairline seemed to recede a little more than the last time Buddy had seen him, and his white dress shirt already had that three o'clock sag. The way Milton leaned forward while rubbing his neck served as a barometer of the situation as he slouched more with each drag of the cigarette.

"You got a violent thief here you need me to shoot or just what is up?"

"I got a little thief for sure but she's not violent. Not yet anyway. She's in the bathroom right now."

"What makes this one so special I couldn't send a uniform to take care of it?"

"It's Millie Franklin, the preacher's daughter."

"Millie? Are you sure she was stealing?"

"Her pockets are full. I haven't checked them yet so I don't know what all she took. I wanted you here before I took this thing any further."

"And you let her go to the bathroom. You know she's probably flushed all the evidence by now."

As he spoke, his words were accented by the loud echo of a flushing toilet on the other side of the door marked Employees Only. That same door opened and a silent, pale, girl walked out and sat down on a box marked "Fragile."

She was teenaged thin and looked even younger than fifteen, lost in her heavy navy winter coat. Her blonde hair was pulled back tight on her head, making her blue eyes look larger than they were. She was frail and cautious but there was something defiant about that sweet, apple-pie face that didn't fear staring you in the eye.

Buddy opened his overcoat and removed his hat from a head of hair so thick and curly it showed no indenture from the brown fedora. He looked around and found a box to sit on that put him on her level.

"Millie," Lt. Briggs said in his best professional-yet-fatherly voice, "what's going on here?"

Millie shrugged as only a fifteen-year-old can.

"Did you take something from the store without paying for it?"

"I reckon."

"Why?"

"I don't know."

"What did you take, Millie? Let me see your pockets."

Millie stood and reached into the pockets of her jacket, pulled out two fistfuls of merchandise and laid them on a packing table. Buddy picked them up one by one. A pair of imitation leather gloves, a pack of bobby pins, two combs, a small picture frame with a headshot of Rhonda Fleming, and a boy's ID bracelet. The whole mess came to less than twenty dollars. At least we were talking about petty larceny here. "Petty" made it sound good. "Larceny" made it sound bad.

"What were you gonna to do with this stuff, Millie?"

"I don't know."

"You don't know? Didn't you have something in mind when you pocketed these items?"

"I reckon."

"Millie," Milton interrupted, "I don't want to cause you and your family any trouble, but if I don't press charges, I could lose my job."

Buddy cut his eyes at Milton with a look that said, "Shut up and let me handle this."

"Millie," Buddy said, leaning over and looking her in the eyes, "have you ever done this before?"

"Not really."

Buddy rifled through the merchandise again. "Who're the gloves for? You? They're about your size. Do you really need bobby pins and combs and a picture frame that bad? And this bracelet. This is not for you is it?"

"They aren't for me. They're Christmas presents."

"You got any money on you, Millie? Cause if you do, I think we can just walk this stuff up to the cash register and you can pay and we'll all go home and forget all about it. What do you say?"

"I don't have any money. I can get some, but I don't have any with me."

"You can go home and get some?"

Milton broke in again, "I can't do that, Buddy. Too many people already know about this. I could get fired by the home company if they found out I let somebody go just because I know 'em. I can't do it."

"I said I *can* get the money not that I *will*."

"What do you mean by that?" Lt. Briggs' voice was all professional with no hint of fatherly anywhere to be heard.

"Do whatever you want to do with me. I don't care. I'm not payin' for anything. Take me to jail. I don't care." The blue in those young eyes was no longer pretty. Iced and penetrating and hard, but not pretty.

A funeral silence overcame the dusty stockroom and lingered for at least sixty seconds, which is a long time for three people to stare at one another. Lt. Briggs stuffed the pilfered items in his overcoat pockets, then took Millie Franklin by the arm and they walked not out the back door, but the length of the store to the front door and down Main Street until they were both out of Milton Sandridge's line of sight. Customers and clerks alike watched the unlikely couple marching past the toys and kitchen utensils and finally the magazine rack and out the frosted doors. Some were silent, some were smiling, and some were just glad the Christmas season was almost over.

Milton stood in the storeroom doorway, lit another cigarette, and wiped the sweat from his forehead. Thirty-six degrees outside and he needed a cold drink.

CHAPTER

Two days before Christmas as many patients as possible had been sent home from Lenity General Hospital. Some would return the day after, but, for now, the hospital was only a third full and the second-floor waiting room was empty except for two sisters waiting for their father to wake up from his mid-morning nap in room 213. Walter Selman was seventy years of age and in perfect health, except for the flu bug that had hit him a week ago. Routine symptoms turned into something more serious a couple of days later, and he was suddenly facing the threat of spending Christmas morning in a crank-up bed watching a snowy television. He was not happy. As a matter of fact he was more angry than sick to hear him tell it. He mostly blamed his doctor son-in-law for the time he was spending in this antiseptic environment. When he slept, he was happier and more peaceful than he had been in days, but when he awoke, it would be hell to pay all over again for the family that was keeping him here.

Walter's daughters, Colleen Sandridge and Doris Sterrett, were concerned for his health and at the same time a little amused at his attitude. He was a perfect mixture of love and dread in his waking hours.

"Do you think Camp will let him go home for Christmas day?" Colleen asked.

"That's not officially his call. You know, being family, he can't legally treat him as his patient. But he'll get him out if it's safe."

"Where would he go? He can't go home by himself. He'd have to stay with one of us."

"I think it best if he stays with us. That way Camp will be there if he has any setbacks," Doris said.

"But you have your kids. At our house it's just Milton and me, and we have the room. It really is no problem."

"We could always leave it up to him."

"Yeah, that's a good one. Like he's not going to want to go home by himself. When Mamma was alive, she could handle him, but he's going to get mad at us no matter what decision we make."

"Let's wait till Camp gets here. Maybe he'll have a better idea."

The room fell silent and they both went back to reading; Colleen her *Reader's Digest* and Doris her *Look*. The room was silent till Doris finished leafing from the back to the front and laid the magazine in her lap. She looked at Colleen for a long time without saying anything.

Finally Colleen looked up and asked, "What?"

"I'm just wondering."

"Wondering what?"

"Are you okay? I mean is everything all right?"

"Everything's fine. Why do you ask?"

"Hey, you're my little sister," said Doris. "I can tell these things. I've always known when something was wrong."

"Nothing's wrong."

"Colleen, you know what I mean. How are things between you and Milton?"

"Milton is Milton and all is well."

"Oh, I really wish you would have adopted. And it's still not too late. I shudder to think what life with just

Dr. Campbell Sterrett would be like. I love him and all, don't get me wrong. But it could get really ... you, know. The kids make all the difference. Louis Wayne, of course, is practically grown. Did I tell you he made the varsity basketball team again? We were so proud of him. You've got to come to some of the games. The girls go crazy over him. But then you probably already know that. You teachers know everything about everybody. And little Hoyt. He was a blessing coming along nine years later. His big thing this year is Santa. He's beginning to wonder, you know? I say tell him the truth and let it go but Camp wants to keep the mystery alive as long as possible. You know what I'm trying to say? You need something more. Maybe Milton needs something more. I tell you, it's not too late."

"Doris, we're fine. You love your kids. I love your kids. Leave it at that. And as far as that Santa thing, Milton is playing Santa at the store Christmas Eve again this year. From two to four. Bring Hoyt by and I'll tell Milton to give him an extra boost."

"You weren't listening ... as usual. I said I want to tell him the truth."

"Tell who the truth?" Dr. Campbell Sterrett, asked as he

walked into the family waiting room. "When doctors are forced to tell the truth, the whole world is going to be in trouble."

"Hi, Camp. "

"How's my prettiest sister-in-law? And my prettiest wife?"

"What's the verdict on Dad?" Doris stood, showing her impatience and eagerness to leave.

"I think we can take him home tomorrow. Maybe for good. If we get his temperature to stay down overnight, he'll be okay."

"To our house or to Colleen's?"

"Better make that ours. There we always have a doctor in the house."

Colleen smiled at Campbell's feeble attempt at a joke. Doris sneered. Things were almost back to normal.

"Let's go see if Dad's awake."

Walter was awake and everyone one on the second floor knew it. His TV blasted at full volume, the blinds were open wide, and he was in high gear. He looked up and saw his two daughters and his son-in-law come through the door.

"When am I gettin' out of here?"

"Hi, Dad." Colleen kissed him on the cheek.

"How about tomorrow … if you're willing to come home with us and behave yourself?" Doris asked.

"Tomorrow is one day too late but if that's the best I can do with the connections I have, then so be it."

Campbell smiled and held his tongue.

"Dr. Yandell will have to make the official decision," Doris added before Campbell had a chance to retort.

"That little bandicoot. He ain't got no more business being a doctor than Hoyt does ridin' a bull. He told me two days ago I had pneumonia. Then it was bronchitis. Now he's gonna send me home. I oughta just get up and go right now. And I would if I knew where my pants were."

"There's a pair in the closet, but I'll bring you some more clothes in the morning or Milton can bring them tonight when he comes."

"Yeah, tell Milton to do that. I may want to go to the cafeteria and eat supper. Milton will take me."

The temperature fell two more degrees outside and ten more in Walter's room as Doris gathered her coat and she and Dr. Sterrett headed down the hall. Colleen stayed and fluffed Walter's pillows and his spirits.

CHAPTER

It was Millie's first ride in a police car. Though Buddy had made her walk the length of the store, an obvious attempt to shame her, he decided to save her the humiliation of sitting in the backseat, behind the screen. He figured facing her daddy would be humiliation enough.

"Millie, if there is anything you can tell me that can save us from having to go through with this, do it now. Do it, if not for yourself, for him. He doesn't deserve this."

"How do you know he doesn't deserve it?"

"What is that supposed to mean?"

"It means whatever you want it to mean. I don't care what you tell him."

The car stopped in front of the house by the church, and Buddy turned off the engine. They sat there for a few moments, neither one of them saying anything. Buddy looked at her and saw a girl almost as old as his own daughter. A girl in trouble. A different kind of trouble to be sure, but so defiant. When he opened the car door, he said it as a warning and also to show her who was in charge: "I'm not gonna tell him anything, Millie. You're gonna tell him."

The Rev. Paul Franklin opened the door after just one ring. If he was shocked at the pair standing on the porch, his face didn't betray it. Buddy, as good as his promise, never spoke a word. Words were rarely necessary when parents opened the door to discover their child standing beside a police officer.

Rev. Franklin simply said, "Buddy," as a greeting and motioned with his left arm for them to come inside.

In the study Paul sat behind his desk, and Buddy and Millie sat in the chairs facing him like a couple begging a loan from a bank president.

"Paul, I think Millie has something to tell you."

She looked up from staring at the carpet to her dad, then over to Buddy and back to her father. Her stare never faltered.

"They caught me stealing from Macalbee's. Mr. San-dridge called the cops and here I am. He wants me to tell him why and you're gonna want me to say I'm sorry and I don't plan to do either so I'm going to my room." And she left.

It was a toss-up as to which side of the desk looked more uncomfortable. Both men were in a business to take charge but neither wanted to use their work strategy against the other.

"Has anyone pressed charges?"

"No."

"Do I need to write you a check for what she took?"

"No. We got it all back. Do you want to know what it was?"

"It doesn't matter. That she took it is what matters. And I think I know why."

The study door opened and the considerable good looks of the preacher's wife filled the room.

"Hi, Buddy. What's going on?"

"It's Millie. They caught her shoplifting at Macalbee's. Buddy just brought her home. She's up in her room."

"Who turned her in?"

"Why?"

"I want to know who turned her in."

"Milton called and asked me to handle it," said Buddy. "I think he's willing to keep it as quiet as possible as long as his home office doesn't find out about it."

"Calling the cops is not exactly keeping it quiet!" Dove Franklin exploded with the fervor of a defensive mother. "How do we know she was actually stealing?"

"They caught her red-handed, Dove, and she admits it. What more could you want?" Paul Franklin, man of God, looked as tired and gray as his Perry Como sweater.

"Well, I would want someone to show a little more consideration than to bring her home in a police car."

"I'm sorry, Dove, but that's the only car the city gives me. I could have walked her up the hill but it's a little cold out there."

Dove left, slamming the study door behind her. Buddy rubbed the backs of his hands for a few seconds before he spoke. The preacher was staring at his desktop.

"I'm sorry about the car in front of the house, Paul. I can come up with a story if you need to tell the neighbors something."

"I don't need any excuses for the truth," the preacher said with sad eyes. "You're looking at a man who struggles with the truth every day. It's comes with the job."

"Yeah, but I guess other people's truths are easier to deal with than your own, and I'm sorry I had to be the one to lay all of this at your doorstep."

"I'm used to it. She's not a bad girl. She just wants to *be* a bad girl."

Paul Franklin fingered a brass paperweight shaped like a cross and considered an unspoken explanation of what he was feeling. He knew his daughter was of an age where she longed for an identity all her own. Maybe she didn't want to be the minister's daughter anymore. He could remember a time a few short years ago when she was so proud of her daddy and would sit on his lap while he wrote his sermons each week at this very desk. Once, when she was six, he overheard her delivering a sermon to her dolls and stuffed animals lined up on her bed. But now her friends were the most important things in her life. Did she want them to think she was as wild as they were? He was afraid to answer. He already had evidence that she smoked and drank, and now he could add stealing to that list of questionable behaviors. What else might she do? Maybe she was just a normal, curious teenager stumbling through these awkward years doing the best she could. He looked up at the man on the other side of his desk and found his voice again. "She's fifteen. She knows all the answers to all the questions you and I are still wrestling with. She even thinks …"

Paul stopped in mid-sentence when he saw tears in Lt. Briggs' eyes. What had he said that would have extracted this kind of reaction from this rock-hard war hero?

"Buddy, what's the matter?"

Buddy took a moment before he answered. "If I hadn't come here today because of Millie's situation, I would have been here for another reason. Everything that's happening is hitting me right in the heart. I've got a problem and Amanda will probably kill me for telling you without consulting her first, but … well, I know you've got a lot on you right now and this is probably the wrong time to unload on you …"

"If you have something you need to talk about, my friend, now is as good as any time to do it. I'm here for whatever you need."

"Amanda called me about an hour ago just before I left the office, so I really haven't had time to let it all soak in, but she had just found out that Shirley Ann is going to have a baby."

"Your Shirley Ann? Your sixteen-year-old Shirley Ann? God have mercy on us all. Tell me all about it."

"I just told you everything I know."

CHAPTER

Amanda Briggs was sitting on the sofa with her legs curled under her, drinking coffee and stroking her daughter's hair. Shirley Ann was lying on the sofa, her head in her mother's lap. Shirley Ann's eyes were red and swollen from crying. Amanda just stared out the picture window at the wind gusting snow flurries across the lawn.

"Did you tell daddy yet?"

"Yes, I did. I told him on the phone just a little while ago."

Shirley Ann began sobbing again. Her mother's stroke on her hair never faltered.

"What did he say? And tell me exactly. Was he mad?"

"He wasn't mad."

"Did he cuss and yell?"

"No. He was very calm. He was busy and I don't think it all sank in at the time."

"Is he coming home?"

"I don't know. He didn't say."

"Mamma, I am so sorry. I don't know what to do. All I knew was I had to tell you. I'm sorry that it hurt you and I hope you don't hate me but …"

"Honey, I don't hate you. No one hates you."

"Daddy will."

"No, he won't. He knows how to handle … unexpected things. He does it every day."

Shirley Ann wondered if her dad had asked who the father was. Her mother asked earlier but Shirley Ann said she wasn't ready to say. Shirley Ann knew she would have to tell them soon. She knew when she'd confided in her mother that it would all come out eventually. She couldn't put it off forever.

"Honey, I know this hasn't been easy. But there are some things I have to ask. You may as well talk to me before your father comes home. It will be easier that way. I was sixteen once. I know. Talk to me now while it's just us."

"Okay."

"How long have you been seeing this boy?"

"It's been going on since summer. We haven't really dated in public because he has a girlfriend and I have Tommy, and we've sort of kept it a secret."

"So when did you see one another?"

"I would tell you I was going downtown to meet Tommy and then I wouldn't. I'd go meet … him. Sometimes I'd say I was over at Kathy's and I wasn't. I'd be with him. He has a car."

"Shirley Ann, if you want me to see you through this thing then you're going to have to start treating me like someone you trust. Like you treat your friends. You're going to have to level with me. Do you understand?"

The weather dropped another five degrees and the wind whistled around the front door. There was no sunshine outside and certainly none inside. The gloom of a gray wintry morning rushed through every window of the living room and Shirley Ann was so long answering that Amanda thought she might have dozed off. But finally with no further urging, the daughter said a name she knew her mother wasn't expecting.

"Louis Wayne Sterrett."

"Dr. Sterrett's son? Have you told him?"

"He knows."

"And?"

"He's going to tell his parents tonight. We both
wanted to wait till after Christmas but I just couldn't do
it. I just couldn't get all through Christmas with that on
my conscience. And he agreed."

They both stiffened as they heard car tires on the
gravel driveway. Shirley Ann began to sob again, not
in fear, but in the shame she knew she'd feel when she
looked in her father's eyes. They waited for the kitchen
door to open but it never did. Instead, someone knocked
at the front door.

Shirley Ann sat up and pulled her hair back and
wiped at her face, hoping to magically erase the redness
and puffiness for whomever was at the front door. Amanda
walked across the room spreading the wrinkles out of her
dress with both hands and reached the door as the anxious
visitor pushed the bell for the second time. She opened
it, and there stood the father of her unborn grandchild.
Tall, scared, and handsome. There was no other way to
describe him. Amanda thought maybe she should add
brave, because it took a lot of nerve to ring that doorbell.

As a fellow human being she wanted to shake his hand. As a mother she wanted to wring his neck.

"Mrs. Briggs, I'm Louis Wayne Sterrett. Is Shirley Ann home?"

Amanda Briggs gave Louis Wayne the same old silent, one-armed wave-in that Paul Franklin was giving her husband right at that moment, although she had no way of knowing it. Louis Wayne stepped in and Amanda closed the door behind him and found Shirley Ann standing in the middle of the room in equal parts shock and elation. Her prince had come to her rescue.

"Mamma, this is Louis Wayne."

"I know who he is. Sit down."

"Mrs. Briggs, I guess you know why I'm here.…"

"No, no I don't. I know what you've done, but I don't know why you're here."

"I'm here to lay claim to what I've done and I don't know any better way than to do it face-to-face."

Amanda Briggs would remember that little speech many years to come and would repeat it often for all who would listen. It was a character-sketch-in-brief of a young man and who he was and what he would become. Amanda

Briggs wasn't shy and neither was Louis Wayne Sterrett, and she liked that. She liked him in spite of what he had done to her daughter and to her family. He had a lot of man in him for a seventeen-year-old, and she only hoped Buddy would see the same qualities she was seeing.

"Mr. Sterrett, this family is in turmoil because of you."

"I know that, and while I'm not proud of what has happened, I am also not ashamed and I'm not going to let anyone else be ashamed because I love your daughter and I want to marry her."

"Louis," Amanda said, shortening his name to match her temper, "you are both in high school. How are you going to marry this girl and raise this baby?"

"I have a part-time job now, and after graduation I can go to work full time and on top of that my family has money."

Amanda wanted to fire a sharp and biting comeback but could only focus on his honesty. She was afraid Buddy would see it as cockiness.

"I'm going to make some lunch. You're welcome to stay. You might as well eat with us. You're practically family."

"Yes, ma'am, and I'm looking forward to the day I will be."

But just as Amanda got to the kitchen door, a flash of anger hit her. She turned and spoke sharply to Louis Wayne. "If you're so in love with my daughter, why did you have to sneak around for the past four months instead of dating her like a girl should be dated?"

"That's a hard question. Do you want the truth?"

"If you've got the truth in you, son, I want it."

"I was dating Barbara Suter, coach's daughter, and I knew if I broke up with her, he'd cut me from the team."

"Well, you can be sure he's going to cut you now."

"Yes, ma'am."

"You want Pepsi or Dr Pepper?"

"Dr Pepper."

CHAPTER

There is nothing worse than waiting in a hospital bed for a meal not worth waiting for. It was getting colder outside by the minute and the wind was racing across the parking lot as fast as the gloom was racing into Walter Selman's room. His daughters and son-in-law were long gone and he was alone with his memories and his dread. He was hoping all he had was a bad case of the flu, and yet he was surprised at how calm he was when he wondered if it might be something much worse. Life comes in stages and when each stage leaves, it takes a hunk of the soul with it. Large hunks of Walter's soul had left in the past quarter of a century. When his daughters left home for college. When they married. And, of course, when Ella died.

What was left of his soul cared mostly for memories.

Thank God, they were mostly good. Tomorrow would be Christmas Eve and most memories of past Christmas Eves only got sweeter with each passing year. The Christmas trees and open-house parties. Sneaking in toys after midnight. Eating Santa's cookies and getting up before anyone else in the house to turn on the tree lights on Christmas morning. The snow flurries. The arrival of last-minute packages. All these things brought a smile to his lips as he looked out the window into the dark and listened to the sounds of nurses in the hallway.

Then there were the flowers. The flowers were foremost in his mind tonight. They always were on Christmas Eve. And then he drifted, not off to sleep, but back fifty-four years to the Christmas of 1904. The wind on the parking lot became the wind around the marquee of the Crown Theater, and the sounds of the nurses became backstage chatter of stagehands and actors. It was just hours to show time.

The winter of 1904 had not been easy. The few automobiles that traveled the streets in Mt. Jefferson had given way to the horses and carriages that were better prepared for a thirty-day accumulation of snow. Hard rubber tires were no match for Dobbin's hooves. The streets were just as full of day shoppers as ever, and the nights, illuminated by gaslights on each corner, were becoming more popular in spite of the weather. Wilson's Haberdashery was doing record business without putting anything on sale. Train sets were on back order at the Merchant Mart Department Store, and parents stood in line to order more. Lucky's Barber Shop was open till 10 p.m., and any restaurant or cafe that closed before ten missed out on hungry, paying customers. Downtown was a flurry of commerce and color, bursting with red and green from every store window. And the holiday season was good for the Crown Theater, too.

The Crown, barely four years old, sat majestically on the northeast corner of its block and lit up every store within three doors. The café and the furniture store directly across the street had taken to turning off their front lights at night because the glow and spillover from the marquee was sufficient for their evening business. The music hall, as many referred to it early on, was an instant landmark. Although Mt. Jeffersonians swarmed to the performances from the beginning, many had yet to enjoy the Crown experience. That's why the proprietor was happy to light up his corner of the street. The more light the Crown gave to shoppers, the more they would be tempted to peek through the large glass doors at the red and gold carpet in the lobby and the brass railings along the dark paneled walls. The right show would eventually get everyone through the in-swinging doors and turn curiosity into a theater-going habit.

Madge Turner and Her Merrymakers played two shows a day for the first three days of the week. Thursday the theater went dark in anticipation of the biggest play of the season on Friday and Saturday: *The Nativity* performed by a troupe from Baltimore called The Royal Players Group and starring the up-and-coming husband-and-wife team of Nicholas and Adrienne Knoles. Tickets went on sale the day after Thanksgiving and sold out in seventy-two hours due to the large church-going population of Mt. Jefferson and the showmanship and marketing techniques of E. G. Selman, owner of the flourishing Crown. The stage was set, and dress rehearsal was about to begin Friday afternoon for the 8 p.m. performance, which would be repeated again at a 4 p.m. Saturday matinee, a week before Christmas Eve.

The supporting cast waited on stage for their stars. Adrienne and Nicholas Knoles stood in their basement dressing room in full costume. Simon Croft, second lead, playing Herod and all the angel parts, paced in his damp cubicle, listening through an air vent to the conversation on the other side of the cement wall.

"Nick, you know we're late. Let's just do this and then we'll talk all you want and about anything you want."

"I want to talk now. I don't give a rat's hair about the play."

"Don't be a fool. We have a rehearsal and two shows to do. After Christmas we only have half a week in Frederick and then we can talk about what's in our future."

"Our future? My future. That's what I want to talk about. What's in my future?"

"I'm not going to talk about it now and that is that. So shut up about it and let's go to work."

"Give 'em the Virgin Mary, Adrienne. So exemplary to your public. So perfidious to me. You're good, my dear. You're real good. And I'm the biggest fool who ever lived."

"If you want to stay here and pout you can do it by yourself."

Simon Croft wanted to intervene. Should he get involved now or wait and see where this fight was going? He decided to wait until after dress rehearsal before doing anything. Walking into a husband-and-wife spat could be dangerous. Especially this husband-and-wife team. He had seen them unleash their wrath at directors and stage managers and each other more than once. A knock on his door told him he was due on stage in five minutes. He put out his cigar, pushed the blond hair from his eyes, and looked one more time at his image in the cracked mirror. The costume was a little soiled around the collar and the wings and the hem of the white robe was beginning to show dirt from being dragged across the boards, but all in all he looked like an angel. What he felt inside was a different story, and that was the story that concerned him most.

Something crashed suddenly in the room next door. It sounded like a water pitcher breaking against the wall and was followed by a scream that had to be Adrienne. Simon grabbed the doorknob, jerked it open, and ran to the Knoles' dressing room and was nearly knocked down as Nick brushed past, heading for the stage. Simon glanced through the open door and saw Adrienne cowering in the corner, glass around her feet and water drenching her costume. He stepped toward her, but she stopped him.

"I'm all right."

"You have glass in your hair. Here, let me comb it out."

"No. I can do it."

"One of these days he's going to really hurt you. You've got to do something … or let me do something."

"I'll handle it." She began to brush, and as the glass fell from her hair, tears fell from her eyes. Simon turned toward the hallway and said something under his breath she couldn't hear. A voice from upstairs yelled, "One minute."

"Let's take it from the scene where Gabriel has just appeared to Mary and she's frightened and the angel speaks to her. Simon, start with your line."

Gabriel: Hail thou that art highly favored. The Lord is with thee. Blessed art thou among all women.

Mary: Who art thou who comes to me? Is this a dream and am I fast asleep, seeing heavenly visions?

Gabriel: You see no visions, Mary. I am here.

Mary: Then what are these words you speak to me? That I am blessed among women?

Gabriel: Fear not, Mary, for thou has found favor with God.

"I think that's enough rehearsal for you two," Nicholas' voiced boomed as he walked onto the stage. "You know your lines. You know your marks. And, besides that, you're making me sick. Let's go to scene three where I come in."

Adrienne turned and looked at Stoddard, the director, but she knew her silent plea was in vain. He was as scared of Nicholas as everyone else. He hung his head and said, "You might be right, Nick. Let's move on to three."

Adrienne walked off the stage. Simon followed her and grabbed her by the arm, but she pulled away.

"No, Simon. Leave it alone."

"I'll have it out with him right now. I'm not afraid of him."

"I know. But I am."

"Mrs. Knoles, watch your step. It's dark on these stairs. Here let me hold your robe."

"Thank you, son."

The stage boy helped Adrienne Knoles down the stairs to her dressing room, holding the hem of her costume in his right hand and her elbow in his left. He was close enough to smell the perfume on her skin and see the fear in her eyes. He wasn't sure what it all meant. He only knew he wanted to comfort her. As they walked steadily down the steps, her arm felt soft in his hand, yet cold. She was so much smaller the closer he got and so much prettier. He could tell she was upset but he didn't have the words to make her feel better, so he just walked her quietly to her door. As he opened it, she thanked him and went inside and closed it gently.

He stood in the hall for a few minutes listening to her sobs, knowing they had everything to do with her husband, who had been so brash and hateful in front of the cast and crew. He was certain there was more to her sadness but it was not his place to ask. There was no comfort a sixteen-year-old boy could offer, so instead of following his instincts and knocking on the door, he followed his good sense. Walter walked away.

CHAPTER

Millie wasn't lying on her bed facedown or sitting on the edge staring into space or looking pensively out the window as one might expect from an over-dramatic fifteen-year-old. She was standing in the middle of the room with hands on hips, waiting for her mother to knock on and open the bedroom door. Dove Franklin did just as she was expected. First came the knock then the door eased open, revealing her soft voice, "Millie? It's mother."

Millie didn't shout any of the expected responses like "What do you want?" "Come in," or even "I don't feel like talking to you." She just stood there as the door came toward her and her mother eased through the smallest possible opening as if to keep a world full of germs from entering behind her.

"Millie, what is going on? What happened at Macalbee's?"

"They said I stole stuff."

"Did you? Did you shoplift something?"

"I was going to pay for it. I was just picking things up and I was going to pay for it all and then a song came on the loudspeaker and I got to listening to it and I guess I just forgot and sorta walked out the back door without thinking. The next thing I knew they were all over me and telling me I was going to jail and I didn't know what to do."

"Did you tell them that you just forgot? Did you tell them exactly what you're telling me?"

"Exactly what I'm telling you. But they didn't care. That woman with that tight little perm, Mrs. What's-her-face and a little colored man grabbed me and held me and drug me back inside. They took me to some dirty warehouse room and made me wait there on the police."

"Lois Pence. Is that the woman?"

Millie nodded her head.

"Did Mr. Sandridge show up? Was he one of the people who talked to you?"

Millie stared out the window and twisted the chain

she wore around her neck and brushed at flecks that weren't on her sweater.

"Millie, I asked you if Mr. Sandridge was there."

"He was there all right. He was the one that called the cops."

"Honey, why don't you take a bath and lie down for a little bit and let's just let this thing calm down. I'm sure in a few hours it will all look a whole lot different."

Dove said this with her arm around her only daughter and a tear in her voice. But there were no tears in her eyes. Crying was not one of Dove's weaknesses and certainly not one of her defenses. She never even used her striking good looks the way other women who looked even half as good often did. But one glance in her dark brown eyes would have told you her mind was working overtime. She was planning her actions and Millie's excuse and the other side to Paul's inevitable argument. She slipped out of the room as carefully as she slipped in and saw Buddy Briggs walking out the front door to his car as she was coming down the stairs.

"Do you want to bring her down or do we need to talk first?"

"I see no need for either. She's going to bed for a while and I think the best thing to do would be to leave her alone."

"It's not just about the shoplifting, Dove. Do you know what kind of problems she's facing?"

"Problems? In her life or yours? Are you concerned because your daughter has been accused of something she may not have done or are you upset because the 'preacher's kid' is in trouble, and God forbid anything besmirch the preacher's name?"

"That's not fair and you know it."

"Fair is doing all you can for your family. That's what fair is. Not selling out. Not settling down and giving up. Fair to your daughter is giving her every opportunity in life that you can. You think fair is praying for the bull not to trample you, and I think fair is shooting him between the eyes so that he won't ever trample you or anyone else. But what's the point of talking about it? Are we ever going to agree on anything again?"

There was a long silence as she put on her coat and scarf and gloves and he rubbed the backs of his hands and took a deep breath.

"Dove, I'm ready to make that move. You win. You and

Millie. I'm ready to go. Let's just get through Christmas and New Year's and come the first of January, I'll make the calls. And maybe then there will be some semblance of peace in this family again."

"Yeah, you do that," were the last words he heard before the front door slammed shut.

Paul and Dove Franklin had lived in Mt. Jefferson for nearly ten years. For half of that time she had ridden him almost daily to move. She quickly tired of the congregation and their "petty concerns," as she was wont to call them. She never felt a part of his life and the things he felt were important. The people he felt a dedication to, she only felt resentment for. More often than not she viewed his caring nature as a personality flaw. She longed for him to be more concerned about her and Millie than with the one hundred or so pew-fillers he considered his family. What kept her awake nights was that she once felt the way he did. She was long past praying for understanding about why she'd changed. Life changes, and there was nothing she, or anyone else, could do about it.

Dove first saw Paul standing behind a podium from the second row at a campus rally their junior year in college. She fell in love with his authority and command before she even considered if he was cute. Those very traits that drew her to him now drained her daily of any emotion she ever felt for him. Authority and command be damned. She wanted a warm body to talk to and touch and feel close to. She was tired of sharing him with every old maid, divorcee, and new widow in the church who called at suppertime in tears wanting him to come by and listen to their problems. She was tired of interrupted vacations to come home for funerals or sudden hospitalizations. She was tired of being married to the entire church and always, always coming in last where need and desire and a little consideration were concerned.

Paul knew this. He had known for the past seven years. They left his first church about the time Millie started school. That move was for all the right reasons. Bigger church. Bigger community. More money. Better schools. Closer to her parents. But it all got too pat too quickly. The more the men and women of the congregation loved Paul, the more they resented her. Or maybe it just seemed so. She was dissatisfied and had to blame someone for her discomforts. Either way, it was time to move on, but Paul could be just as stubborn as she. And yet maybe he meant what he said. Maybe he was ready to make a move. Did he really want to or was the pressure finally getting to him? Her pressure. Her authority and command. It didn't matter. Being gone was all that would matter. Being gone was the only thing that could solve the problem before it got any worse. The problem no one else knew about. The problem she certainly hoped to God no one else knew about.

Paul stood at the foot of the stairs in the foyer deciding whether to go up and talk to Millie or return to his study and finish the Christmas Eve sermon he had started. If he went upstairs, Millie surely wouldn't talk to him. But if he went back to his desk, his mind would be too cluttered to write anything sensible. For the second time today he wished he still smoked.

Paul gave up all his bad habits the year after he met Dove—the year he decided he was going to seminary. She was his biggest supporter then. She encouraged him and told him often he was making the right decision. When did that stop? When Millie was born? When they moved to Mt. Jefferson? When he quit discussing his decision to stay or look for a new church? It was about that time she stopped teaching Sunday school and singing in the choir. About that time she started telling him how restless she was for a new town and new faces.

Having to make a choice between Dove and his church was something he'd never considered. Not until just a few minutes ago. There was something in her voice this time he had never heard before. He knew right now, two days before Christmas, that he had to make a choice. And he also knew there really were no options. Just one thing to do. The right thing. For the first time in years he felt a certain peace just knowing what was most important to him.

CHAPTER

Christmas was on the cusp in Virginia. The flecks of snow hitting the windshield were beginning to freeze. It wouldn't be long before the streets turned white. Up north people thought it was always sunny and tropical in Virginia. In the Deep South many didn't distinguish between Virginia and West Virginia and thought it was always bitter cold like in Minneapolis. But it could be mild or miserable.

Buddy Briggs was miserable.

Sitting in his car waiting for the engine to warm up before turning on the heater to avoid the gust of cold air, he was trying to decide whether to go back to the station and eat his brown-bag lunch or go home. Without actually deciding, he and his car headed for home. Just as he pulled up in front of the ranch-style home he and

Amanda had built a few years before, a strange car backed out of his drive and drove off in the opposite direction. He parked in the carport and sat there a few seconds. When he walked through the door, he would have to leave the policeman in the car. He needed to be all daddy and husband to handle this situation apart from the rancor boiling inside him.

He opened the kitchen door and saw them sitting at the dinette table. The two loves of his life. Out of habit he slipped the holster off his belt and put it in the first drawer on the right. They were staring at him, waiting. They were as surprised as he was when his anger and frustration melted into tears running down his cheeks. He dropped into a chair at the table. They cried silently together.

"Where do we, ah, start?" he finally said.

"I think we should …" Amanda began to speak, but Shirley Ann interrupted her.

"I'll tell him, Mamma." She looked at her daddy and her tears dried up and she was suddenly the young woman in charge she was going to have to be from now on.

"I'm sorry, Daddy. I know you must hate me right now and I understand if you do. What I did was wrong but what has happened is not wrong. I love him and I want this baby, even though I know it won't be easy."

"Wait," Buddy said with his hand up and head down. "Who is this 'him' that you love so much?"

Shirley Ann continued to look her father in the eye and said, "Louis Wayne Sterrett."

"The basketball player?"

"Dr. Sterrett's son." Amanda interjected a more respectful identity to the young man she had just served lunch. Buddy wasn't impressed. He sat still looking into Shirley Ann's eyes waiting for more.

"We've been seeing one another since this past summer. And, Daddy, before you ask, I know how serious this is and I know what I want. I want to finish this semester and have my baby and then go back and get my diploma maybe next year."

Asking the hard questions was second nature to Buddy. He did it every day with suspects and vagrants and jailhouse regulars. Quizzing and lecturing his only daughter about curfews and morals came easy. But sitting across the kitchen table from a sixteen-year-old who was about to make him a grandfather was the most awkward situation he had ever faced.

Anzio was a card game compared to this. Maybe he couldn't leave the policeman in the car. Maybe he needed some of that part of him to get through the next few minutes.

"How far along are you?"

The little girl wrestled control from the young woman across the table and all she could do was swallow.

"She's two months," Amanda answered.

"Has she seen a doctor?"

"No. That's the next step. We need to do that just as soon as possible."

"Then it's not definite." Buddy grasped for a thin hope that all this might be just a bad dream.

"It's definite, Daddy. Trust me."

"Bad choice of words, honey. Trusting you is how we got where we are right now." Buddy hated himself for the words before they left his lips. He stood up and went to the bathroom to loosen his tie and wash his face.

The only sound he could hear above the running water was more sobbing coming from the kitchen.

Buddy wiped the water from his eyes and looked at the face in the mirror. When did little Buddy Briggs get to looking like this? When did the hollow jowls take over the chubby cheeks and the bright blue eyes take on that dim blue haze? He could remember when forty two years old was an old man. His father was only ten years older than that when he died. Ten years. Is that all he had? His grandson would be in the fifth grade when he was fifty-two. Only ten years he'd have with him. Or her. Maybe this was the blessing he was looking for. Maybe this was why all this was happening now—so that he would have at least ten years with his grandchild. He always thought he would die young. But this wasn't about him and his father. This was about two teenagers raising a child of their own. His daughter and some doctor's son who would probably never step foot on the altar. He had learned this much being a cop. A perpetrator will say whatever he has to at the time.

He was so caught up in his image in the mirror and the possibilities of a rich-kid snob being intimate with his little girl that he didn't hear the bathroom door open and close. He didn't know he wasn't alone until he saw Amanda's reflection. She sat on the edge of the tub. He never turned around. He just reached for her and they held hands for a moment before either spoke.

"He was here."

"Who was here?"

"The Sterrett boy. Louis Wayne. He knocked on the door and came in like he'd been here a thousand times, and I have to tell you, as much as I wanted to kill him on the spot, he handled himself like a man. I'm glad you weren't here, but if you had been, you would have been impressed with him."

"Impressed with him? You sound like you approve of him and … and all this."

"No, Buddy, I don't approve. But I accept what I have to accept and make the best of it. I learned that from you. When you left for service and I was pregnant, it wasn't what we wanted, but we made the best of it."

"You weren't sixteen."

"No, I wasn't. But I could have been. What kind of angel were you at sixteen?"

He turned and looked at her without the benefit of the mirror. But he had nothing to say.

"What if I had been sixteen when you joined up? Would you have changed anything? If we failed some-where along the way, we're going to have to admit that to ourselves and continue on with our heads high. We can't change what has been done. We can only make the best of it. And the best of it is that our little girl is going to grow up faster than most and look life in the face sooner than most, and we have to be there to help her. We can get mad and feel sorry for ourselves all we want, but tomorrow we're going to be another day closer to the truth and the truth is we're going to have a baby in this family."

"So we sign for them to get married and make like nothing ever happened?"

"No. Not like nothing ever happened. We just handle it. And as far as getting married, well yes, I guess we do."

The phone rang in the living room. Amanda said she would get it and Buddy was glad.

"If it's the station, tell them I'm not here."

"Hello."

"Amanda, I have to talk to you."

"What's wrong?

"Are you by yourself?"

"Buddy and Shirley Ann are here. Why? What's wrong?"

"That's okay. I'll talk to you later."

"Dove, what is it? Where are you? I hear noise in the back."

"I'm in a phone booth on Towne Street. But if you can't talk, I'll call later."

"Dove, this is not a real good time but I can tell something's not right. Please tell me what's wrong."

"I'm sorry I called at a bad time. I'll call you later this afternoon. Really don't worry about it. I'll talk to you later. Good-bye."

CHAPTER

The house was quiet when Doris got home at eleven thirty. Hoyt was next door with the Collier kids. Good neighbors are a blessing especially when they have twins the same age as your youngest. You can call it playtime instead of babysitting and free yourself whenever you need to. Doris made a mental note to return the favor over the holidays. But right now she would take advantage of the late-morning stillness, turn on the tree, wrap a few gifts and eat lunch by the television set while watching *As the World Turns*. Oakdale and the Hughes family were a welcome diversion to everything going on in her life. Christmas was coming down like the snowstorm everyone on the radio was predicting. Her dad was in the hospital. Her sister was acting like everything was fine when she knew everything wasn't. Milton wasn't worthy of her sister's love, and she knew something was going on. What, exactly, she wasn't sure and she wasn't even sure Colleen knew. But she would find out. Just as soon as Christmas was over and the dust settled on this thing with her dad, she would find out.

The grilled cheese sandwich was just coming out of the skillet when the side door opened. She expected to see Louis Wayne coming back from wherever he had been all morning, but to her surprise her husband walked in.

"What are you doing here? I thought I just left you at the hospital?"

"Well, you did. But I needed to come home. Sit down a minute. I have to talk to you."

"What?" she asked refusing to sit.

"Sit down."

"Campbell, what has happened?"

Campbell took a seat and spread his hands across a Courier and Ives Christmas placemat. "Just sit down and listen to me. You had no more than left the hospital when Dr. Yandell paged me. I met with him. Doris, it's not pneumonia or bronchitis."

"Don't tell me. Please don't tell me." Her legs demanded she do what her fear had not let her do before and she fell heavily onto the chair, dropping the sandwich on the table.

"You had to know this was a possibility from the very start."

"No. No. No, I didn't have to know anything. You're the doctor in the family. You had to know. You've known all along." She spit the words out of her mouth like shards of glass. Her husband was to blame for this horrible news because someone had to be. The sick anger in her stomach was telling her to strike out at someone close.

Campbell kept his tone steady. "I only had suspicions. Jerry Yandell wasn't sure until the tests came back just an hour ago."

"Does Dad know?"

"Not yet."

"Who's going to tell him? Who's going to tell Colleen? Does she know?" Her mind raced with all that had to be done as she glared across the table at the man who always loved her, in spite of her moods or accusations.

"No one knows anything yet. And I'll tell him if you want, or Jerry can tell him. He's Jerry's patient."

"Who's going to tell Louis Wayne and Hoyt? What are we going to do?"

"I'm going to give you something right now to calm you down." He took out a small bottle of pills and put one in her hand.

"I need to see him." She stood up suddenly.

"No, you don't. We'll tell him first, then you can see him."

"How long does he have? What am I saying? I can't believe I'm saying that. How long?" She was pacing and frantically ringing her hands while holding on to the little blue pill her husband had given her.

"That's a judgment call, honey. No one can be sure." Doris didn't buy his evasive answer. She didn't repeat the question. She just stared at him stone-faced until he responded.

"More than a few months. Less than a year. That's the best I can tell you without going into all the details, which I will if you want me to."

"No. No, I don't want you to. I don't want to hear it. That's all I need to know. I need some wine to take this pill."

"I think not. One or the other but not both."

Doris couldn't cry and she couldn't stop her mind leaping from one family member to the other. Who should she call first? Colleen. It had to be Colleen and then the boys. Thank God Hoyt and Louis Wayne weren't home.

"Will you tell the boys? I'll call Colleen."

"There's time for all that. I know you have to tell Colleen but let's consider telling the boys after Christmas. Why overload them with bad news now? There is no urgency here. Plus it will give you time to digest it."

"You're right. You're always right. You make me sick with always being right. Now get me a glass of wine to take this pill."

Colleen had always been Walter's favorite daughter. Doris knew this and understood why, but she didn't know what to do about it. As a child Doris had tried to please him with piano recitals, ballet reviews, blue ribbons from horse shows, straight As, perfect attendance in everything she undertook, and even giving her firstborn his middle name—Wayne. She always felt she had to work to get his attention but it seemed to come natural to Colleen. They had a bond nothing could break. Every mistake Colleen made, Walter thought was cute. If the teacher sent a note home saying she hadn't done her homework, Daddy would send a note back saying they were overloading her. If she wanted to quit the Girl Scouts or the basketball team, that was fine with him because they were riding her too hard and keeping her too long after school. Colleen was sweet and never knowingly took advantage, but she just did what she wanted and Walter approved. When Doris would complain to their mother, she would say, "Now, now, Doris. Don't be jealous of your little sister." But she was. She loved her. She just resented how their father never saw flaws in Colleen but seemed to look for them in her.

Doris took no pleasure in what she had to do because she, like their father, fell under the natural charm of Colleen and didn't wish to hurt her. She had to be the one to tell her, even though Campbell could do it better. After all, he was a doctor and this is what he did. He cured people and when he couldn't cure them he broke the news to them. And then the next day he did the same thing all over again. She used to wonder if this would harden his heart against the sensitive things in life. She wondered this for years, and when she honestly told herself the truth one day, she realized that he was the same loving man she had married long ago. It was she who had hardened her heart because she wanted to be strong like him. The more she tried to be like her father and her husband, the more she became someone the neighbors didn't like. Why didn't the world welcome strong women? Show a little strength and people think you have a heart of stone. But enough of this. She had to call Colleen.

CHAPTER

Hospital food tends to taste like the trays they're delivered on and Walter Selman was tired of eating metallic meat loaf. The only dessert ever available was green Jell-O, and that reminded him of Jack Benny, whose radio show was sponsored by Jell-O, and that reminded him he had no radio in his room. He missed his radio. He missed Jack Benny who was no longer on the radio, but anything on the radio would be better than those daytime television dramas where the men wore ties all day and the women wore pearls—even in the kitchen. At least Jack Benny was funny. He had seen Jack Benny once in Cleveland. He got an autograph and picture with Mary Livingstone. The name of the theater escaped him. But then they all looked alike where he'd met them—down in the catacombs. The dressing rooms and corridors. All cement and mirrors with doors that didn't lock so actors couldn't pass out drunk between shows or hide from management. That's how it was in the old Crown where his father had booked every major and minor act since the turn of the century. And every time Christmas Eve sneaked up on him, he remembered the Crown and the plays and the music, but mostly Adrienne. Poor, sweet, lovely Adrienne.

Walter didn't want to leave Adrienne alone while she was crying so he sat on the steps outside her dressing room and pretended to repair a wooden cane he had collected from the prop room. He studied the cane and imagined it would be a good weapon should her husband come back to cause her any more trouble. He decided right then and there that he wouldn't let anyone make her cry again. And as he thought this, the sounds on the other side of the door, just five feet away, grew soft. He heard the rustling of cloth. Then the sound of leather soles on the concrete floor and then a sudden stifled scream. He looked up and down the hallway. He couldn't ignore it. He went to the door and put his ear against it and said, "Mrs. Knoles? Are you all right?"

The door opened and he saw the prettiest smile and the whitest petticoat he had ever seen, not that he had seen many petticoats. She opened the door for him to come in seemingly unconcerned about her state of undress.

"I'm sorry. Yes, I'm all right. I just cut my finger on some broken glass. I'm sorry I scared you. Can you get me something to wash it off with? A towel and some water."

"Yes, ma'am. I'll be right back."

And he was.

Adrienne Knoles was sitting at her dressing table gripping a bloody finger with her other hand and looking a little fainter than when he had left. He knelt beside her and washed the blood into the cloth until there was no more. She looked down at him and asked, "What's your name?"

"Walter. Selman. My dad is the theater manager and owner."

What Adrienne did next sealed the moment forever in Walter's mind, a memory never to be forgotten. She leaned down and kissed him on the forehead and said,

"Thank you, Walter. You're the only gentleman I've met today."

The red from her lips didn't show up until the blush went away. And my, how a sixteen-year-old boy can blush. Before he could get up off his knee, someone pushed through the half-closed door.

"What is going on here?"

Walter turned to see a tall blond angel in white flowing robes. Simon Croft. He jumped up, but before he could turn, Croft grabbed him by the collar.

"Simon, what has gotten into you? Leave the boy alone. He was helping me...."

"Helping you? What could he be helping you with?"

"I cut my finger. And the boy was washing the blood off."

"Well, I'm sorry, boy. No, I mean I really am. But, ah, run along now."

Walter, relieved to be unhanded by the angelic giant, never said a word. He picked up the pan and towel and went out, and Simon Croft closed the door behind him. From the hall he could hear low whispering in the room and it was only then that he had the sense that there was more going on between them than rehearsing lines. This made him angry but he wasn't sure where to direct his anger. So many young and misunderstood emotions raced through his heart. He was angry at Simon for being close to her and Adrienne for allowing it. But he couldn't blame Simon Croft for wanting to be close to Adrienne, especially after the way her husband treated her. Knowing right and wrong is easy but placing the blame is a job for the saints.

He started up the steps toward the backstage and met Nicholas Knoles on the stairs. Fear shot through him from the scowl on the actor's face. He turned and watched him walk toward the dressing room he shared with his wife. And to this day he doesn't know why he did it, or where he got the courage to do it, but he stopped at the top of the stairs and yelled, "Mr. Knoles! Mr. Knoles!"

Nicholas turned, not six steps from the closed dressing room door and said, "What is it, son?" His voice was so warm and so gentle Walter almost abandoned his just-thought-of plan. Nicholas Knoles was a different man than the one he watched explode on the stage earlier in the afternoon.

"Mr. Knoles, the stage manager is looking for you. He wants you back up here to go over something."

Nicholas looked puzzled. "I was just there."

"I know, sir, but he's hollering for you."

"Hollering for me is he? Well, you tell him … no, I'll tell him myself. I'll shut the little serpent up. His attitude this entire trip has been …" His words trailed off as he rushed up the steps with venom in his eyes, pushing past Walter in pursuit of an unsuspecting stage manager.

Walter ran back down the steps and knocked on the door of dressing room number one. There was a pause, then Adrienne Knoles said, "Yes?"

"Mrs. Knoles," Walter offered in his loudest whisper, "your husband is coming."

She cracked the door and said, "Thank you, Walter." Simon squeezed out of the opening and walked briskly down the hall to dressing room number two.

Walter disappeared to the prop room and Adrienne softly closed her door.

As he sat in the semi-dark and cold amid old and musty furniture, wooden swords, and cheap paintings, he tried to unravel exactly what was going on with the troupe of *The Nativity*. The way Nicholas Knoles talked to his wife was foreign to him and the way she seemed to cower from him one minute and stand up to him the next confused him. He assured himself he could take comfort in the fact that Adrienne had a good friend and capable protector in Simon Croft. Simon was big and muscular and seemed to really care for her. He was sure Simon would never let Nicholas harm her.

The hall was quiet again.

CHAPTER

The walk from the phone booth to the front doors of Macalbee's was a little more than a block. There was only one side street to cross but she never looked either way. How dare a green light hold her up? How dare a shopper crowd her path? How dare a car get in her way? She had no time for interruptions. She was on a mission and she was focused on one thing and one person only. The cold wind that swept in as she flung open the large glass doors had little to do with the wintry gusts and the dropping temperatures. Dove Franklin generated her own icy rush as she made her way down the oiled wooden floor to the back of the store through a Christmas throng that seemed to part for her in respect and fear of a woman with a purpose.

Milton sat at his desk with his back to the window that looked down into the store. Lois Pence was standing to his side at the adding machine and facing the window. She sensed more than saw Dove Franklin come through the front door and watched with wide eyes and open mouth as she stormed down the aisles.

"Mr. Sandridge. We have trouble again."

"What is it this time? If it's another shoplifter, just shoot her from the window and be over with it."

"I don't think a bullet will stop this one."

Milton straightened up and rubbed his neck with both hands. "You're going to make me look aren't you?"

"Yes, sir. I think you'd better."

Milton turned and took in the scene that hypnotized his assistant manager. The preacher's wife was making a beeline toward the door that would bring her up the steps to his office. He never took his eyes off her as he spoke to his assistant manager.

"Go tell her to come up."

"Do you want me to come with her? It may be good for both of us to be here."

"No. I'll handle it. You stay on the floor. And tell

Ernest to get that Santa suit out of the trunk of my car.
Just put it in the storeroom."

"Yes, sir. And are you sure you don't want me to—"

"I'm sure, Lois. I'll be fine."

Lois left to meet Dove. Milton closed the blind on
the window and poured two cups of coffee. One with
sugar. One with cream.

The door opened but there was no cold rush. The
walk through the warm store had taken the scent of
frigid air out of her clothes and the redness out of her
cheeks. The scarf that had been tied over her head hung
loosely around her shoulders. However, the fire in her
eyes remained. Milton walked around the desk and
reached out his hand to her. She paused for just a second
and then reached out hers and pulled him toward her
into a passionate kiss.

"You unforgivable, rotten …"

"And I love you, too."

"What did you do to my little girl?"

"How about what your little girl did to me? She put
me on the spot with the home office. If they ever find out
how I handled that whole thing this morning …"

"And just how did you handle it? She told you she just forgot to pay and you still called the cops on her."

"Wait a minute. That's not how it happened at all. She filled her pockets and took off out the back door."

"Oh, come on, Milton. She told me the whole story. She told me she offered to pay and you wouldn't hear to it. You called Buddy and he searched her and then brought her up to the house to shame her in front of Paul. What do you want from her? You want to send a fifteen-year-old girl to jail?"

"Yeah, Dove. That's it. You caught me. That's what I do. I sit up here and watch out that little window and try to find kids I can send to jail. And if I can do it just two days before Christmas, then I really get a bang out of it."

"Okay, if that's not the way it happened, then what did happen? Are you saying Millie lied to me?"

"I'd say yes, there's a pretty good chance Millie is lying to you. If one of us has a reason to lie to you, I'm betting on her. You can't exactly take my television privileges away or ground me for two weeks or stop my allowance. So, yeah, I'd say Millie is probably lying. And believe me, she has reason to. She walked in here this

morning and filled her pockets with junk and then talked
as defiantly to a policeman as, I don't know, as a criminal
on *Dragnet* or something. Maybe you *should* take some
television privileges away from her."

"You don't have children. If you did, you might see
this differently. You might see everything differently."
Dove was sitting now, her coat off and sipping the sugar-
only coffee. She felt more at ease than she had all day.
Maybe Milton was telling her the truth. Maybe Millie
had done it on purpose and for a purpose. It certainly
wasn't hard to figure out why she might do such a thing.
It's shocking, she thought, what some people will do for
lack of attention.

Dove and Milton had been high school sweethearts.
They grew up together just a couple hours east of Mt.
Jefferson, in Richmond. The summer following their
senior year found them making plans to go their separate
ways even though they were both distraught over their
separation. Dove was heading to college to follow in her
sister's footsteps, and Milton was joining up to do his

naval duty in the Pacific or Atlantic. It was a sad summer of songs that still haunted, memories that still lingered, and promises that never came true. They had loved one another as deeply and sincerely as two sixteen-year-olds could, and they meant it from the depths of their young souls when they pledged to always be together after she'd graduated from college and he'd returned from his tour of duty. They held each other that summer and told one another they could weather anything that came their way because they always had the promise of a future together. They would see one another during spring and Christmas breaks as furloughs allowed. Then they would meet in Richmond at the end of their obligations and live happily ever after. Theirs was a special love. A special relationship that neither time nor space could mar.

But time and space did mar it. The spring breaks and Christmas vacations didn't match up with the furloughs. The miles between took their toll. The telephone to a love affair is as satisfying as the smell of roast beef is to a hungry man. By the time college was over, Dove had found the man she needed—a man of authority and more tellingly, though she didn't admit it to herself until years later, someone convenient, someone available and nearby. She needed someone who would be there to hold her and comfort her and make love to her. Letters and phone calls couldn't do that. Milton, who had not tried quite as hard as she, felt the same way and knew that what they were trying to do was inhuman. He blamed no one for the end of their dream. It was the hand life had dealt them and, sad as it may be, he knew they would be all right. The young and strong always are.

Milton was never serious for any other girl until after he was transferred to Mt. Jefferson. He had gone to work for Macalbee's in Richmond after the service and after a few good promotions had bounced around the state as assistant manager a number of times. He was glad to finally be offered a store of his own. He came to town a bachelor on the prowl and met Colleen Selman, a schoolteacher, just months after arriving. The promotions didn't stop coming but he stopped the promotions. He liked Mt. Jefferson, and all other towns paled in comparison, so he turned them down until the home office finally quit considering him. He chose to be stuck in Mt. Jefferson. And he liked it. Especially now.

Ten years ago the Mason Street Methodist Church

hired a new minister from Kentucky, and he brought to town with him a pretty little five-year-old daughter and a beautiful wife who turned everyone's eye. Having lost track years before, Milton was as shocked on that first Sunday morning as was the lovely and unsuspecting Dove. They looked at one another longingly and shook hands dutifully and went their separate ways that afternoon, never saying a word to anyone about the other. It was weeks before opportunity, be it chance or kismet, found them alone in an empty hallway in the basement of the church.

"Are you alone?" Dove asked.

"Yes."

"Can you believe this?"

"What has happened? Has God played a big joke on us or what?"

"Maybe he's testing us."

"I hope not because I don't know if I can pass the test or not," said Milton. "How have you been?"

"Just fine, I suppose. And you?"

"I'm still in shock over this coincidence."

"How long have you lived here and how long have you and Colleen been married?"

"Lived here a couple of years. Been married about a year. She's a wonderful woman, and I love her. But I've loved you all my life."

"Milton, don't say that."

"I didn't say anything wrong. I just told you the truth. Just because we lost track and never saw one another, does that mean you forgot about me?"

"What it means is that I am now the Mrs. Rev. Paul Franklin. I am a mother and a wife and sing in the choir and it feels good. You ought to try it."

"What? Singing in the choir?"

"Yeah, if you want to."

"If you're going to, I will. That way I'll get to see you every Thursday night."

"Milton, seriously …"

"I am serious."

"Seriously, have you said anything to anyone at all about you and me and that we knew each other back when?"

"Only that we went to school together. I figured we shouldn't lie about that. Why? Have you."

"Just that we went to school together in Richmond."

"Why not more? Why haven't you said we dated in high school and were lovers and planned to get married one day?"

"Why haven't you?"

And that was all they said about it. They protected themselves and one another through instinct and friendship, and it was a long time before they found themselves alone again. On the few occasions they did, they rekindled what had been, not physically, but emotionally. And they were both thankful for their restraint. It wasn't until years later that they started stealing planned minutes in hallways and half-hours in cafes in out-of-the-way places outside of town. There they talked and often kissed and felt closer to each other than they did to anyone else in the world. They were in love without making love. They knew God wouldn't be proud of them for their choices, but believed He would have to give them a gold star for effort.

Dove removed her shoes and was curling her legs up to sit on her feet when the phone rang. Milton reached across the desk and picked up the receiver.

"Hello."

Dove could only hear one side of the conversation, but she could tell by the look on his face, the quickening of his back, the timbre of his voice, that it was Colleen. She liked Colleen. And the more she liked Colleen, the more she disliked herself. What she was doing with her husband wasn't right. It could be *more* wrong, but it wasn't right. She sat quietly not knowing if she should tiptoe out or say out loud, "Tell Colleen I said hi," and pretend she was here on a friendly visit or on a mother's fact-finding mission for an errant daughter. This was too much to consider so she just continued to sit very quietly and sip the cooling coffee that was growing more bitter with every taste.

When Milton hung up the phone, he set it down into the cradle very slowly and took his time before saying anything at all. Dove waited, giving him the time he needed.

"That was Colleen."

"Yes, I figured it was."

"Walter's sick."

"I knew he was in the hospital."

"No, I mean sick. He's only got months to live."

"Oh, honey, I'm so sorry. Does Paul know?"

"She's calling him now." There was a long pause. "I'm sorry. I'm not thinking real clear. I really like the ole guy."

"I know you do. I'll go so you can do what you have to do. You need to go home and be with her."

"Yeah."

Dove got up and put on her scarf and coat and gloves. Milton walked to the door with her and she turned and kissed him good-bye on the cheek. As she opened the door he said, "Don't worry about that thing with Millie. She's just a kid going through a kid phase. She'll be okay."

"She's not who I'm worried about right now. Are you going to be all right?"

"I've made it through two wars and twenty years without you, Dove. I can make it through anything."

She closed the door and Milton walked back to his desk and opened the blinds on the store window. The aisles were full. The shelves were getting empty. The day was getting longer. Walter was dying. Colleen was crying. Dove was walking down aisle three. And Christmas was only two days away.

CHAPTER

The Sterrett house sat at the end of Whitman Drive. It was the first house in a brand-new development that would see magnificent growth in the 1960s. The doctor and his wife, Doris, built it before their last child was born in 1951, and it is still the flagship of residences in a neighborhood of beautiful homes. Every Christmas the stone wall and the driveway are illuminated by rows of multicolored lights that will stay up till New Year's Day. On Tuesday, December 23, 1958, at 2:00 p.m., the Sterrett house showed no signs of the season, as the lights would not come on till dusk. Louis Wayne turned into the lane and parked under the carport by the kitchen door. He sat under the wheel and listened to the last verse of "The Chipmunk Song." Simon, Theodore, and Alvin might be the last laugh he would have for a while. He turned off the engine and went inside.

His mother and his father were sitting in the living room drinking hot tea, Campbell on the sofa, Doris in her wingback chair. The house was silent. Louis Wayne walked from room to room until he found them. The living room was never used except for company and special occasions. *Well*, he thought, *this was certainly a special occasion*.

"What are you two doing in here?"

"Oh, hi, Louis Wayne. Come sit down. Where have you been?"

"Out doin' stuff. Are you okay, Mother?"

"She's fine. Just a little tired. Where's Barbara? Is she with you?"

"No, she's not. Just me."

Louis Wayne thought it strange his mother had still not said a word. He knew it was going to be an awkward conversation but he didn't expect it to be this uncomfortable before he even started.

"Are you guys busy? Have you got a minute?"

"Always, son. What's on your mind?"

His mother looked sedated, but Louis Wayne knew this was no time to stop and change the subject. He'd been riding around for the past hour working up the courage and forming the words. He had to keep going or he would find all kinds of reasons to back out.

"Pop, Mother, I have something pretty serious to tell you. I don't know how to go about it so I'll just do it. You asked about Barbara. Well …"

"Have you two broken up?"

"No. Well, yes. I guess we have broken up. But that's not what this is about." Louis addressed everything to his father. "Pop, I have been seeing someone else. And I'm in love with her. I know you may think that's just something I'm saying, but I really am. Shirley Ann Briggs. That's who I've been seeing."

"Pretty girl. I know who she is. Cheerleader isn't she?"

"Yeah."

"Have you broken the news to Barbara?"

"It's more than that. Just let me finish." The words started coming slower and with more difficulty. Each word stretched out into a sentence. "I. Have been. Seeing her. For quite sometime. We're in love. Very much in love. And we're going to have a baby."

The silence of the house when he first walked in sounded like a football game compared to this quiet. The glass of red wine his mother had been holding slid out of her hand and rested on its side in her lap. A dark stain spread on her gray wool skirt, but she didn't seem to notice. And if his father was still breathing, there was no evidence of this. Then the only movement and sound that defied the stony silence came a moment later when his mother leaned forward in her chair and vomited all over her legs.

"I have to go back to work."

"But you haven't said what you think about tonight."

Buddy and Amanda Briggs were standing outside in the driveway. He was wearing his coat and hat and she wore a sweater around her shoulders and was hugging her arms close to her body. The snowflakes were still fine and melted when they hit the pavement, but it wouldn't be long before they started to stick.

"I don't know. Whose idea was this again?"

"Shirley Ann's and Louis Wayne's. It's the way they want to do it. I think it's a good idea."

"Do I have any choice in the matter?"

"Buddy, you can say yes and go with us or say no and stay home."

"Do we know that the Sterretts want this? Are they going to want us there or is this just something Shirley Ann and the boy have come up with?"

"The boy has a name. Get used to it."

"Is this just something Shirley Ann and that wonderful young man Louis Wayne Sterrett came up with?"

"Oh, Buddy, go to work."

"What do you want me to do, Mandy? You want me to go over there and hug this boy and thank him for knocking up our one and only daughter and tell his family how terrific I think he is? You want me to kiss each one of them on the lips and wish them a Merry Christmas? Is that what you want me to do?"

"What other choice do we have? You tell me another way to handle this and I'll listen. I'm just trying to make it easy on everybody concerned. Now you can get mad and take weeks or maybe months to come around, but you know you will come around because there is nowhere else to go. You love your daughter. If you don't, if this has turned you against her for life and you can just send her out in the cold and never see her or your grandchild again, then … well … I guess you'd have to live with that. But if you know that eventually you're going to come around and be the man I know you are, then you might as well skip all that hotshot stuff and start tonight."

Buddy sighed heavily and looked up at the gathering clouds. "Yeah, I'll come around. But I just don't know if I can do it tonight. I may need a little more time."

He got in the car and started the engine but this time he didn't wait for it to warm up the heater. He just backed out the driveway and turned toward town.

Amanda stood there in the snow not feeling the cold. She needed a little time too. She was doing more talking than feeling for the sake of Shirley and the benefit of Buddy. But she knew she would feel the weight of her feelings soon enough. She walked back in the house and put her sweater on a chair, turned on the radio and began washing dishes. The Christmas music didn't sound the same. Early this morning it had lifted her spirits but now even Bing Crosby couldn't cheer her up. She forced herself to hum along to "Silent Night." And by the time the dishes were dried and "Blue Christmas" ended, she sat down at the table and put her head in her hands and started to cry. Immediately the phone rang. The voice on the other end had always dried her tears.

"Mandy. I'll go tonight. I'm ready."

"I love you."

"What's there about me not to love? I'm a pushover. I love you too."

She put the phone back in the cradle and began to hum along with "The Little Drummer Boy." She was already beginning to feel better. With Buddy on her side, she could face anything. Even Doris Sterrett.

CHAPTER

The door to room 213 in Lenity General Hospital opened, and a small dark man in a dark blue suit walked out into the corridor. He stopped and said something in a low tone to a nurse on duty and then proceeded down the hall toward the elevators. Dr. Jerry Yandall had just told Walter Selman that the day after tomorrow he would celebrate his last Christmas on earth. He also told him he could go home tomorrow morning if he wanted. And then he had told him that if he wanted to speak to a minister, priest, or rabbi of his choice, he would arrange it.

Life went on as usual outside room 213. The snow was coming in spurts, and the cars driving by were in a hurry to get where they were going before the streets turned to ice. Inside room 213, Walter Selman was doing what he had been doing for the past week. Lying in bed and thinking. To his credit, his thinking wasn't much different this afternoon than it had been all week. He wasn't sad. He wasn't heartsick or destroyed. He was quiet with maybe a hint of relief. He was old enough to know that dying was not the worst thing that could happen to a man. Lingering and laboring and longing could be so much worse and he wasn't prone to these. He sensed no change in his disposition or mood. He was enjoying the solitude and worried only that his family would worry. Maybe he didn't still have his health, but he still had his memories and as long as a man has memories, he isn't dead. Walter was as alive in this moment as he was before Dr. Yandall gave him the news. Where was the sting? Not here. Not now. Not yet. He still had Christmas. He still had the flowers. He still had his memories.

It was thirty minutes till showtime and young Walter was in Hansen's Drugs and Notions down the street from the Crown. On orders from his father he was to bring steaming mugs of coffee to the principals thirty minutes before the curtain went up. Walter was about to cross the ice-slick street with a box containing three cups of black coffee when someone grabbed him by the arm, almost spilling his delivery. It was Simon Croft.

"Boy, do you have a doctor around here close?"

"Yes, sir. Just up there," Walter motioned with his head toward a house leading up the hill on Market Street.

"You better get him. I'll take that coffee. You go get him and bring him to my dressing room."

"What's wrong? What's happened?" Simon Croft had scared him but it scared him more that something might be wrong with Adrienne.

"Mrs. Knoles got a cut on her head and somebody needs to look at it before she goes on."

Walter quickly handed the box of coffees to the actor and asked, "What happened?"

"Are you a doctor, boy? Just go get him and tell him to get here fast. We go on in twenty-five minutes."

Walter ran the short distance to Dr. Butler's two-story brick house and banged on the front door with the brass doorknocker. No answer. He peered through every window from the front porch and saw no sign of light or life inside. He ran out to the front walk and yelled for the doctor five or six times but still got no response. He turned and ran back toward the theater, almost getting trampled by a horse and buggy and falling down twice on the ice. He ran to the stage door and burst through and raced down the concrete steps, stopping breathlessly at dressing room number two. He knocked frantically till Simon Croft cracked the door open and peeked out.

"You got a doctor?"

"No. He wasn't home. What's wrong?"

From inside he heard Adrienne's voice say, "Let him in."

Simon stepped back slowly and reluctantly held the door open far enough for Walter to slip through. The light was dim inside but he could see the outline of Adrienne Knoles sitting in a corner with her hand to her head. He walked over to her and saw she was holding a wet cloth to her face.

As if he were in charge, and he sort of felt he was, he took her hand and moved it away from her face and saw a bruise above her left eye. He wanted to ask a dozen questions but he didn't. It was fifteen minutes to eight, and he knew there was no time for answers.

"The skin isn't broken. Does it hurt?" he asked, sounding much older than his sixteen years.

"My whole head hurts. Aches all over."

"It's not bleeding. Can you go on?"

"I can go on but how am I going to explain this?"

"Where's your makeup kit? We can cover it with lots of makeup and you wear a scarf most of the time, don't you?"

"I suppose so."

He could tell Adrienne wasn't thinking clearly or she would already have thought of these things. And where was her husband? Did he know how badly she was hurt? Or had he just hit her and left her and didn't care?

Walter, working under the pressure of time, doctored the wound, helped to apply the makeup, tied the scarf at an angle, and stood back and was pleased with what he had done. He was about to take her by the arm and stand her up when the stage manager knocked on the door and yelled, "Five minutes."

Simon Croft had been no help at all. He was cowering in the corner in full costume, smelling of fear and alcohol. Walter realized that he was as weak as he was big. This man, whom he had earlier thought was the perfect protector for Adrienne, was crumbling in front of him. A friend, maybe; a protector, not a chance. He took Adrienne by the arm and said to Simon Croft, "You walk up the steps on one side of her and I'll take the other side."

"What if we run into Nick?" Simon said to both Adrienne and Walter. Walter could see he was afraid and wasn't even ashamed of it.

"If he's in his dressing room, we're okay because he's not in the first scene. He won't come up for another ten minutes." Walter didn't really know more about the play than these two actors; he was just thinking more clearly than they were. He opened the door and looked down the hall. He took Adrienne to the steps and held her right arm while Simon held the left. Anyone watching this scene would have surmised the star was simply getting the star treatment. And in all honesty she was.

The show that must go on went on, and the audience loved it, and they loved Adrienne. The audience stood and shouted for her to take bow after bow and tossed flowers on the stage. Adrienne smiled and bowed like a professional and it wasn't until the crowd finally began to disperse that she collapsed to her knees in the wings and had to be carried to her dressing room by two stagehands who had no idea what was going on. But then neither did Walter.

CHAPTER

Millie Franklin was watching the snow from her second-floor bedroom in the Methodist manse. She was enjoying the jazzed-up version of "White Christmas" by the Drifters that poured out of the radio, but that didn't matter because her mind was filled with thoughts that kept her from catching the holiday spirit.

Shirley Ann Briggs was watching it snow from her bedroom as "White Christmas" by the Drifters played in the background. She didn't like the way they jazzed it up, but that didn't matter because her mind was preoccupied with the all the changes that soon would engulf her life.

Louis Wayne Sterrett was watching the snow fall through the French doors of his bedroom. He didn't know if he liked or disliked the way the Drifters had jazzed up "White Christmas," but that really didn't matter with everything that was going on downstairs in his living room. His father was on his knees cleaning the carpet and his mother was passed out on the sofa. They had agreed to invite the Briggs family over to talk and to get to know them. He told his parents how much he wanted them to meet Shirley Ann, and he felt it might be best to meet Lt. Buddy Briggs in the relative safety of a crowd. He wasn't looking forward to that at all. He wished his granddad could be home by then. Granddad could control his mother and intimidate his father and diffuse the most explosive of situations. He could put things in perspective like no other. Maybe he would see him this afternoon at the hospital.

It was already three thirty, and time was running out with all the things he had to do. He decided to call Shirley Ann and tell her the family conference was on for seven thirty. He'd have plenty of time later to talk to his granddad.

"Hello."

"Dove?"

"Hi, Amanda. I'm glad you called."

"Well, I was concerned about you. Sorry I couldn't talk earlier. What's wrong?"

Dove Franklin lowered her voice. "I would feel more comfortable talking about it in person. Could you meet me somewhere?"

"I guess. How bad are the roads?"

"The snow's stopped so I think they're okay."

"Shirley Ann is in her room. She'll be okay here for a little while. Do you want me to come there?"

"No. Let's meet … at … how about Beecher's?"

"Across from Macalbee's?"

"That's it. How about in fifteen minutes?"

As Dove was heading for the front door, her husband walked out of his study.

"Going out again?"

"I'm going to meet Amanda Briggs for coffee."

"Who will be here with Millie? I have to go out in a few minutes myself."

"She'll be all right. She's fifteen. She's not a baby."

"No, but we're going to have to start watching her like she's a baby."

"Paul, I talked to her and I told her she was not to leave the house. She knows she's being punished. She will stay in her room. You go do whatever you have to do and don't worry about it. I'll handle it."

Rev. Franklin turned back into his office and said as he walked, "I'm sure you will, Dove. I'm sure you will."

As the front door closed behind his wife, Paul picked up the telephone and dialed a number he had scratched on a note pad. It rang three times before anyone answered.

"Macalbee's. Merry Christmas!"

"May I speak to the manager, Mr. Sandridge, please?"

"Who may I say is calling?"

"Paul Franklin."

"One moment please."

Lois Pence cupped her left hand over the bottom of the receiver and said, "Mr. Sandridge, it's Rev. Franklin. He wants to speak to you."

Milton's back stiffened and he drew in a sudden breath. He hoped Lois didn't notice as he swiveled slowly around toward the outstretched phone cord and reached out his hand.

"If you need me to be a witness to that girl's stealing, I will. I'm not afraid of him."

"I'm not afraid of him either, Lois. Just give me the phone." His voice was tired and heavy.

Milton spoke in his best managerial tone, "Paul. How are you?"

"I'm fine, Milton. I'm calling to tell you how sorry I am for all the trouble my daughter has caused you. I'm embarrassed and discouraged over it and certainly ashamed of her actions."

"Paul. Please. Say no more. We can handle this quietly. Don't be embarrassed or ashamed. She's just a kid who did a foolish thing. It happens every day."

"It doesn't happen to *me* every day. This was a planned and premeditated offense. Those are the hardest sins to forgive. They're also the ones that hurt the most. And if she did it once, she is likely to do it again. People often repeat the same sin over and over until they get punished for it. Then more likely than not they're sorry for being caught instead of sorry for what they did. Do you know what I'm saying, Milton?"

"Yes, sir." Milton answered as if his father were talking to him.

"I'm coming down to see you."

"No, that's okay. You don't have to do that."

"I think I do. We need to talk. And we need to see eye to eye when we do. I can be there in the next half hour if that's suitable to you."

"Paul …"

"Yes?"

"Nothing. Sure. In a half hour will be fine with me."

Beecher's was a coffee shop and soda fountain from another era. The small white tiles on the floor and the dark oak paneling on the walls were holdovers from the turn-of-the-century occupants, Hansen's Drugs and Notions—a store that had been there for nearly sixty years. But the soda fountain wasn't the main attraction. Above the fountain was an enormous mounted moose head with antlers that reached at least four feet into the air. On the left antler hung a black tattered top hat, said to have been tossed there by a past mayor who had stopped in one night for a bicarbonate of soda after a night at the opera at the old Crown Theater. On the right antler hung a white, silk lined scarf, turned yellow now with time, its legend lost to the ages. Both icons remained for decades and had become such a part of the town history that when the drugstore changed hands and was turned into a coffee shop and fountain, they stayed on as part of the local color. Dove and Amanda sat near the front window at a small table for two.

"The reason I called this morning was because of Millie. She's really done it this time. They caught her shoplifting over at Macalbee's about ten o'clock this morning."

"*They* caught her? Who are they?"

"Yeah, well, you're right. *Him.*"

"What happened? I mean, I am so sorry for Millie. But what did they do and what did she take? I don't know what to ask first here," said Amanda.

"She apparently just walked in and started picking things up and putting them in her pockets...."

"What kind of things?"

"Oh, I don't know. A pack of bobby pins. A picture frame. Silly things."

"Why?"

"That's the part that bothers me most," said Dove. "I could go with the easy answer and agree with Paul. He says she did it to embarrass him. To prove that she's not a goody-goody preacher's kid. And there might be something to that. She's had a lot of responsibility forced on her. Everything she does gets magnified because of who Paul is. Lord knows, I feel plenty of that myself."

"But what else? You said that was the easy answer. What else do you think it was?"

"Mandy, you're the only person in the world I can say this to." Rare tears were shining in Dove's eyes and her voice was defying her strength. "I think Millie knows about Milton and me."

"Oh, Dove, no. Certainly not. Why do you think that?"

"He and I went over to Cantersville to eat lunch together a couple of weeks ago and just get away and talk. You know all that. And while we were in this little restaurant, I thought I saw the mother of one of her girlfriends come in and leave real quick. I wasn't sure but I couldn't get it off my mind."

"Who was it?"

"Judy Bowers. Do you know her?"

"No."

"Anyway, she has a big mouth, and I should have gotten up and gone out and got her by the arm and introduced her to Milton and made everything okay right there on the spot, but I didn't."

"You would have introduced her to Milton?"

"I always have a story ready in case someone sees us. I'll tell them we've been to a church conference down the valley somewhere and just stopped in here for a bite of lunch or that we had a committee meeting at one of the local churches and stopped here for coffee. I figure if you're open and act like there's nothing to hide, people will believe you."

"Have you ever had to use one of those excuses?"

"Actually, no. So I really don't know how good I'd be at it. But I sure wish I had used it with Judy Bowers. I kick myself every day for not following her out and talking to her. We must have looked awful guilty sitting there in that back booth at two o'clock in the afternoon twenty-five miles from home. I'm sure she told her daughter and her daughter told Millie. I could almost tell you the exact day she found out because she hasn't treated me the same since."

"And you think that's why she chose to shoplift at Macalbee's this morning? To get back at Milton?"

"Yes, I do. And I think it's time we get out of this town before somebody else finds out more than there is to find out. When we get caught, we're going to get blamed for a full-fledged affair. No one, my husband included, is going to believe what we haven't been doing. We might as well be sleeping together because that's what the rumor is going to be if we ever get caught."

"Don't say that, Dove. Don't say that. Are you serious about leaving?"

"Paul finally agreed this morning to go. I think this thing with Millie was the final straw. And I'm ready. I'm so ready. You are the only person I will miss in this town. The only one. I love you for the friend you've been to me, but I have to get out of here and away from Milton before something happens that ruins all of our lives. Thanks for listening to me and letting me run on and on like this. How about you? How's everything in your life?"

Amanda signaled for two more cups of coffee.

CHAPTER

Walter knew there was very little time before his daughters would be coming through that door. Colleen would try to be all smiles but that wouldn't last. She'd be in tears inside of three minutes. That's the kind of heart she had. Big and soft and easy to break. And then he would wind up consoling her. He didn't mind. He never minded doing anything for his little Colleen.

And then next through the door, probably an hour or two later, would be Doris. She would be mad. Angry? No, mad! She would challenge the doctors and the nursing staff and demand a recount of blood corpuscles and take to task everyone from the orderly to the administrator. She would sweep in shouting orders and put the fear of God in everyone who crossed her path. Pretty little Doris. How he loved her and her take-no-prisoners attitude. But he could never convince her of that. She was always trying too hard; trying too hard to win his love instead of enjoying it. She desired approval over affection. Attention over contentment. Or … she may not come at all. Maybe she would be passed out on the sofa, full of tranquilizers and expensive gin.

Either way, he figured he only had a few moments to himself before the room filled up. A few moments to nap. A few moments to dream. A few moments to remember.

Neither the audience nor her husband saw Adrienne collapse behind the curtain. He was on the opposite side of the stage and never saw her being carried down the stone steps to their basement dressing room. He was busy berating the director for late cue prompting in the second act. When he pushed open the door to their shared dressing quarters, she had already shooed the stagehands out. Nicholas found his wife sitting at her dressing table applying cold cream to her face and neck. He stepped out of his costume, dressed in a pair of woolen slacks and cotton shirt, put on a full-length top coat with silver buttons and a plaid dress hat and left the room without a word.

Walter saw him leave through the stage door and cross the street to the Brennaman House Hotel and disappear through their revolving front door. Feeling assured he was gone for the night, Walter hurried back down the hall to Adrienne's dressing room and knocked gently on the door. Seeing Walter, she walked back and sat down again in front of the mirror leaving the open door as an invitation for him to come in.

"Adrienne, ah, Mrs. Knoles, are you alright?"

"My head hurts. And my vision is blurred out of my left eye. Can you see the swelling?"

Walter stepped between her and the wall mirror to get a better look. The bruise was much worse than it had been a couple of hours ago.

"I think we should let my father look at it or maybe you should go to the hospital."

"No. I just need to sit here a minute. Close the door, Walter, and don't let anyone else in."

Walter moved toward the door but before he could shut it, Simon Croft pushed his way in. He had a cigar in one hand and a bottle of whiskey in the other. He was dressed in his street clothes, and for the first time, Walter noticed an edge in his voice when he spoke to Adrienne.

"You've carried this thing far enough. Get dressed and go back to the hotel and sleep it off. Your head will be better in the morning."

"I think she's hurt pretty bad," said Walter.

"What do you know? Stick to carrying coffee and sleeping in the prop room or whatever it is you do around here. You're not a doctor. You can't even find one when we need one. Why don't you run along home and let us take care of things here, boy."

"Simon." The way Adrienne spoke his name sounded like a scolding. Walter looked at her and then at him. Something was going on that had him puzzled. He suddenly felt very nervous to be standing between these two lovers and his anxiety increased when the door quickly opened and Nicholas Knoles walked in.

"What are you doing in my dressing room?" This question was directed explicitly toward Walter. But before he could stammer an answer, Nicholas turned to Simon and said, "And what are *you* doing in my dressing room?"

Then all of his attention went to his wife. "And what happened to your head?"

This was when it all came rushing to Walter's young senses that he had read this scene the wrong way. Nicholas hadn't caused Adrienne's wound. And if he hadn't caused it, it must have been Simon.

Nicholas knelt in front of Adrienne and pushed the hair away from her forehead and looked closely at the blue bruise that was gathering blood just under the surface of the skin.

"What happened? Who did this to you?"

Before she could answer, Simon started backing toward the door. "It was an accident, Nick. I swear it was. I didn't mean to."

What happened next happened so fast Walter had a hard time recalling it later. Adrienne jumped up from the chair and tried to deflect Nicholas' hand as he reached under his overcoat and pulled a small pearl-handled revolver. It was as if she knew by instinct what was about to happen—as if this scene had been played out before in other towns, in other dressing rooms. With his free hand he tried to push her to the side but she stepped away and yelled for Simon to run and at Nicholas to stop. Neither happened.

The two sounds that followed would ring for years in Walter's ears: Adrienne Knoles screaming "No!" and a single shot from a .38 caliber pistol.

When the reverberations settled, Simon was cowered against the wall with spittle on his chin and eyes closed tightly in terror, a broken whiskey bottle at his feet. Nicholas was standing in the middle of the room empty-handed, his gun lying on the floor. Slumped partially over a straight back chair was his wife, conscious but bleeding from the abdomen.

"Adrienne. Dear God, my Adrienne."

Walter had seen it all. He had seen the surprise in Nicholas Knoles' face upon discovering what Simon had done to his wife. He had seen Simon's poorly disguised deception—an attempt to make Walter believe Nicholas had hurt his wife. And he had seen Adrienne, dear, lovely Adrienne, step between her husband and her lover to take the bullet that was meant for the man who had harmed her; the bullet that was meant to protect her honor; the bullet that just might take her life.

This trio of humanity was puzzling for a young boy. Had Adrienne, his innocent, beautiful Adrienne, the heroine of his dreams, traded one violent lover for another? Simon, who Walter had thought to be her friend, had bruised her face with his own hands. Adrienne must have misread his affections and character. And Nicholas, her acerbic and difficult husband, a man who suffered from an uncontrollable temper, still risked everything—even a murder charge—to protect his wife.

Walter Selman ran from the room to find his father and to find an automobile to take Adrienne to the hospital. It was only a week until Christmas. None of this could be happening.

CHAPTER

"How about a couple of pieces of pie to go with those coffees?"

"I don't think for me, thanks," said Amanda.

"Me either," said Dove.

"We have chocolate, butterscotch, and pumpkin."

"No, thank you."

"We also have a chocolate layer cake that's really good today."

"We're fine with just the coffee," said Dove.

"Okay. Just whistle if you need a refill," and the waitress was off to her duties in the kitchen.

Dove glared at her back till the swinging door she had pushed through was practically still. "There's a thin line between helpful and nosy. I think she's nosy."

Amanda smiled. "Oh, she was just pushing leftovers from lunch. She's harmless. Anyway, you asked about me. Well, I've got a real major mess on my hands."

"You've come to the right place, honey, because I am the mess queen."

"Shirley Ann is pregnant."

"Amanda. You don't mean it."

"Oh, I mean it. She just told me this morning."

"Did you have any idea?"

"That's hard to say. I always thought I'd know. You know how mothers and daughters are and we've always been close. So I thought I'd know. And to be painfully honest, I suspected that something was going on. I thought maybe she was getting a little too involved with Tommy Jarvis, this boy she's been dating. For some reason I put off talking to her about it. Of course, I never thought it had gone this far. Lo and behold, I waited too long. I just waited too long."

"Tommy Jarvis? I'm not sure I know the boy."

"Doesn't matter because that's not who it is. That's who she's been dating but that's not the father. The father is Louis Wayne Sterrett."

Dove put her hands to her mouth, sat back in her

chair, and sighed a deep and needed sigh. "Honey, you *are* the new mess queen."

They both laughed laughs of shared relief as only two good friends who never have to explain themselves to one another can.

The snow flurries picked up outside Beecher's as the conversation picked up at its front table. Dove and Amanda needed each other this afternoon. They were confidants who knew what they said would not go beyond the edges of the small table they were leaning into as they exchanged problems and solutions. After both their hearts had been emptied, and they were about to pay for the coffee, Dove said, "Oh, and something else. Have you heard about Walter Selman?"

"No. What's wrong?"

"He's in the hospital. They've only given him months to live."

"He's such a nice man. What is it?"

"I don't know for sure. I didn't ask. You know when they say only months to live, I usually don't like to delve into it and I guess at that point it really doesn't ..."

"Dove, look!"

Dove turned and looked out the front window.

Through the gathering winter storm, she saw her husband going in the front door of Macalbee's. She turned back to the table and locked eyes with Amanda for just a few seconds. She slowly took off her scarf, raised her hand, and said, "Hey, honey, we'll take two pieces of that chocolate layer cake." And then to Amanda, "I'm not going anywhere. Not till I see him come out of there."

Amanda looked at her watch and wondered if she should call home.

Milton had been watching from his second-floor lookout window for the past fifteen minutes. He was scanning the shoppers on the floor below as he usually did, but the focus of his attention was on the front doors. Paul Franklin would be coming through them any minute and he didn't want to be surprised with a knock on his office door. Why was he coming? He had already apologized for Millie's actions. Why did he feel they should meet face-to-face? What else was on his mind? Had he talked to Dove? That was why he was watching the front door. He would wait until he saw Paul come in the front door, and then, while he walked through the store, Milton would call Dove and see if she knew why he was coming.

And there he was. Paul wasn't ten feet inside the front doors when a woman engaged him in a jovial conversation. Milton quickly dialed the number of the Methodist manse. It rang three times before he heard, "Hello."

"Dove?"

"No. This is Millie. She's not here. Can I take a message?"

This was the second time today Millie Franklin had given him palpitations. He hoped the pause didn't appear as long on the other end of the line as it did on this one.

"No. Thank you. I'll call back." He hung up. As he did, he looked back through the window but couldn't see Paul. He scanned the floor aisle by aisle. He had lost him.

The knock on his office door was like a wrecking ball hitting a condemned building. Milton jumped and yelled more than spoke, "Come in."

"Good afternoon, Milton."

They shook hands and Milton offered the preacher a chair—the same one Dove had sat curled up in just a couple of hours ago. Milton waited.

"I've never been up here. This is a very cozy office you have here."

"Thank you. It's ah … it's okay."

"Are you okay, Milton? You look a little pale."

"I'm fine. Just the Christmas season. You know how that is. Retail at Christmastime. How about you? You okay?"

"Not really, Milton. Not really. I've had a pretty rough day."

"Really?"

"You know some days are made for rest and some for labor and some just for learning. Today, the good Lord knows, there has been no rest and I haven't had much time for labor, but heaven help me, I certainly have learned a lot. I've had things revealed to me today I have been blind to for years. Things I should have seen and should have known; but I was just too trusting to allow myself to give them a thought. You ever had days like that, Milton?"

Milton wished he would quit saying his name. If he was doing it to intimidate him, it was working. The back of Milton's head hurt from his neck to his crown. It was a numb ache. He couldn't remember what the last question was. Was it rhetorical or was he required to answer?

"Yeah, I know what you mean. I sure do know what you mean."

"Milton, we need to settle this. I hope and pray we can put it behind us and never have to face anything like this again."

"Okay." Even though he solemnly agreed with what Paul had said, Milton was unsure what to expect next. When Paul stood and reached in his overcoat pocket, for a flash in time, one he would never forget, Milton wondered in a panic if he was reaching for a pistol. What he removed, though, was a pack of bobby pins.

"Buddy Briggs left these things at my house this morning and said I could pay for them or bring them back. I'll let that be your decision, Milton. However you want to handle it." He set the bobby pins on Milton's desk, then reached back into his overcoat pocket to retrieve the rest of the stolen items: gloves, two combs, an identification bracelet, and a silver picture frame with a color photo of Rhonda Fleming or Jeanne Crain. Milton wasn't sure which. He always got them mixed up.

"What do I owe you, Milton?" Paul asked.

"You don't owe me anything." Milton knew he needed to say something more, but he was out of breath and could think of nothing appropriate.

"I really am sorry about everything, Milton. I wish I

could do something to make it up to you. I feel my entire family owes you an apology. We have interfered in the peace of your Christmas season and caused you undue worry and stress at a most unfortunate time. What can I do for you, Milton? Just name it."

Amanda and Dove were sipping cold coffee when Paul came out the front door and pulled his collar up against the city wind. Dove spotted him first and a sudden twisting in her stomach stopped her mouth from working. She jumped up and grabbed her coat, leaned over and kissed Amanda on the cheek and said as she was leaving, "Thanks, honey, for listening to me. I'm here for you and Shirley Ann and Buddy. I'll pray for you. Sit up with you. Cry with you. Whatever you need—you know that. Just call me. Good luck tonight with that Sterrett family meeting. I'd rather go in the lion's den than Doris Sterrett's den. But right now I need to catch my husband and walk home with him. See ya."

And Amanda was alone. Maybe that's what she would do too—go and see her husband. Maybe they could go home together and pick up Shirley Ann and go out to eat and then, together, head over to the lion's den.

CHAPTER

There is nothing lonelier than a hospital room at dusk with one bedside lamp burning. The clatter and noise in the hall contrasted with the dull silence in the open-door room put Walter Selman, a man caught between two worlds, in a reflective mood. There were many things he wasn't sure of but the one thing he felt certain about was he would eat no more hospital food. Even before he had been visited by that dunderpate of a doctor, Yandy or Yandall or whatever his name was, he had decided to go to the cafeteria for dinner. Milton would be here soon to join him. And while he was waiting, Walter decided to put on a shirt and some trousers. Dr. Yahoo probably wouldn't approve, but who was going to ask him?

Milton was a good man. Walter wasn't sure if Colleen shared those same sentiments with the same enthusiasm, but he was never sure if the two of them were in love. Colleen seemed taken enough with him when they'd first met, of course. But after a year or so he could sense the intensity was gone. It wasn't the kind of thing anyone thinks their father or father-in-law would notice, but he did. Colleen started doing more things by herself. His little girl dropped by the house alone more and more. He watched as his sweet Colleen gave up on having children, and he and Ella knew that had been her greatest dream, her greatest desire. Doris was the one they never figured for kids. She was so career-minded and socially driven. That she took time out of her busy life to give birth twice was always a mystery to her mother and him.

Even when he saw Milton pulling away, working longer hours at the store and going back on Sunday evenings to do bookwork and spending holidays redecorating the front windows, even with all this, Walter never allowed himself to think there was anything seriously wrong with the marriage. He figured they were just settling into comfortable routines. Maybe the passion had cooled, but doesn't it always? Ella wondered something different—something Walter didn't want to believe, but sometimes did. She wondered if there was another woman. "Maybe those trips back to Richmond to the home office weren't business at all," she would say aloud. "Or maybe it was someone right there in the store." He and Ella discussed all the possibilities but never confronted Milton. Once Ella considered talking to the preacher's wife about it, being as how she had known him back in Richmond. But Walter wouldn't let her. He told her there was no reason to involve the preacher and his wife in family business. That's how rumors got started and dirty laundry got scattered all over town.

Even with these suspicions Walter couldn't help liking Milton. Now on the other hand, Dr. Campbell Sterrett had done everything in his power to make Walter love and adore him and frankly the more he tried, the more annoying he found him. Try as he may, Walter just couldn't feel anything for the man. Certainly there was plenty of reason to respect him. He had given him two wonderful grandsons and—well, that was all he could think of. It was enough. That was all Walter wanted from him.

But those things shouldn't have been on his mind tonight. Both his girls were well provided for. He should just be thankful and content himself with the comfort of knowing that even if Dr. Sterrett wasn't as flawed as he often thought he was and Milton wasn't as perfect as he often thought he was, both his girls could have done a whole lot worse.

As he sat on the edge of the bed in the dim, eerie light that the small lampshade muted from most of the room, he nearly jumped at the sudden rattling of the window. The wind was picking up again, blowing freezing snow against the big panes. Blowing cold against the warmth of the room. Blowing memories back again. He didn't have time for those memories now but he didn't have the strength to resist them.

Running from the dressing room in horror, Walter crashed into his father who was rushing toward the screams.

"Dad! It's Adrienne. She's been shot. You have to do something."

E. G. Selman, a big man, grabbed his son and pushed him back into the room. He stood in the doorway and held the boy close while he surveyed the scene. He wasn't prone to excitement, and he observed and calculated before he spoke. His gaze went from Adrienne's body leaning over a chair on to the startled Nicholas who stood frozen in the center of the room with expressionless eyes to Simon who was sobbing hysterically with his head thrown back against the wall. E. G. Selman knelt immediately and took Adrienne's hand and saw that she was conscious and aware. He spoke gently and quickly to her.

"Where's the pain?"

"It's in my stomach. Am I bleeding? I'm afraid to look."

"You're going to be all right. I'm going to get help."

E. G. Selman turned to his son and said, "Come here." He took Walter's right hand and pressed it against Adrienne's stomach near the wound. "Put as much pressure as she can stand right here and don't let up until I get back. Do you hear me?"

"Yes, sir."

"You stay here and don't let go of her for any reason." Then he left in a near run and Walter was again alone with the principal cast of *The Nativity*. He pushed his hand against Adrienne's stomach and felt it moisten with her lifeblood more and more with each passing second. She looked up at Walter and smiled as if to comfort him.

"Walter, hold my hand."

Her cold fingers gripped his free hand with more vigor than Walter was applying to her wound. Her voice was only a whisper, but every word she spoke was clear and demanding.

"Walter, tell Nicholas to get out of here. Simon, too. They don't need to be here when the doctor and the police come. Tell them to leave the theater and the town. Now. Please, Walter."

Walter looked up at Nicholas who was still staring at his wife and the pain he had caused. "Nicholas, she says for you to leave. Now. Get out of town quick. Before the police come. You, too, Simon."

Sixteen-year-old Walter Selman felt oddly in charge. He was giving orders, second-hand orders though they may be, to adults who were unable to think for themselves. He sensed he was doing something wrong, but it was what Adrienne wanted so it couldn't be too wrong. He didn't want to fail her at a time when everyone else in her life had failed her.

Nicholas kneeled and put his hand behind her head and said, "Adrienne, dear."

She cut him off quickly. "Go, Nick. Get away while you can. We'll take care of this. You must go and go now and take Simon with you."

"I'll rot in hell before I take him anywhere. Adrienne, I love you and I won't be far."

With this he left the room, partly in obedience to his wife and partly in relief. He protested little to her demand. Simon was still in the room. She spoke softly again to Walter, "Get him out of here."

"I can't. I can't leave you. I can't let go of you."

"Am I bleeding that badly?"

Walter could tell her the truth and risk throwing her into a panic or he could soften the answer. He opted for the latter.

"It's just that my dad said to keep my hand here. I can't let go."

"Simon," she rasped as loudly as she could. "Run. Do you understand?"

Simon Croft, angel extraordinaire, never heard her. He was glued to the wall. Time was of no consequence. He was dazed with fright and guilt and hadn't moved since the shot was fired.

"Simon!" Walter yelled, surprising himself at his assertiveness. "Did you hear her? Run. Get out of here."

As if the sternness in the boy's voice or the volume of it had jarred him back to reality, Simon turned and slinked out the doorway. Walter turned his attention back to Adrienne.

"Just stay calm. You'll be all right."

"Walter, listen closely to me. This was an accident. No one was at fault. I was someplace I shouldn't have been. No one meant …" A pain slashed through her body and haltered her speech and contorted her face. Then she continued. "No one meant to do this. It was an accident. You've got to be with me on this, Walter. An accident."

Walter didn't want to commit to anything he might not be able to live up to later. But he certainly would try. He nodded his head. It *was* an accident. Nicholas never meant to harm his wife. He was trying to kill Simon. So, yes, it was an accident. That wasn't a lie.

"An accident, Walter."

"Yes, ma'am. It was an accident. Don't try to talk anymore. The ambulance should be here any minute now."

"Walter."

"Milton. Come in. Come in. I was just standing here by the window watching the cars slipping and sliding in the snow. I wouldn't want to be down there, but it sure is fun from up here watching them sloshing through that mess."

"What are you doing dressed?"

"Didn't Colleen tell you? We're going out, you and me."

"Can you do that?"

"Sure I can. We're going to the cafeteria downstairs. You haven't eaten have you?"

"No."

"You're on your dinner break?"

"Yes, but aren't you on some sort of special diet?"

"Yeah. I'm on a roast beef, mashed potatoes, and butterscotch pie diet."

"Are you sure, Walter?"

"What's wrong, Miltie? You think the roast beef might kill me? Come on, Milton, lighten up. It's suppertime."

The two men, father-in-law and son-in-law, with a bond that neither one of them could explain, lightened up and walked out of room 213 with their arms around one another.

CHAPTER

With the wind spitting snow in their faces and people waving hello on every corner, it was a pleasant walk home for Paul and Dove. The last block up the hill to the manse, they held hands just like in their college days. They laughed and talked about packages they had yet to wrap, and when they reached the front porch and wiped the wetness from their shoes, Paul cupped her face in his hands and kissed her cold nose. Dove felt like she had just opened a dozen presents on Christmas morning. She couldn't explain the feeling but she also couldn't ignore it. Paul even helped her with her coat when they stepped into the entrance hall.

Dove fixed supper and they ate in the living room by the television and watched the *Huntley-Brinkley Report*. It was a quiet, winter suppertime with a mood that had been missing for a long time. Millie joined them with her TV tray but nobody said anything about the problem at hand, and Dove was in no mood to bring it up and spoil whatever was in the air. Paul helped her wash dishes and they talked easily about everything and it felt like old times again. Until …

"I need to go to the hospital in the morning. I need to check on two church members."

"Walter Selman and who else?"

"Ethel Cummings. There's a good chance both of them may come home tomorrow, so I'll call before I go."

"Have you heard from either of them today?" Dove was fishing even though she already knew the answer. Or thought she did.

"Haven't heard a word."

"You haven't? You haven't heard anything about Walter Selman?"

"No. Why? What should I have heard?"

"Oh, nothing. I just thought there may have been some news."

Dove was sure Milton had told her that Colleen would call Paul. That was close. She couldn't know about this from Milton. She had to wait until someone told Paul. Where did that feeling go? That Christmas comfort. That suppertime peace with her family. What had happened?

Amanda. Dove had to call Amanda and warn her not to say anything tonight. Why hadn't Colleen called? She made an excuse and ran up the stairs to call from the bedroom phone.

As she topped the steps, Millie came out of her room and said, "You got a call this afternoon but they didn't leave a message."

"Oh. Well, I guess they'll call back."

"Yeah, I guess." And then she went back in her room.

Dove went to her bedroom and closed the door. She dialed the Briggs' number and let it ring seven times. *They must have already left for the Sterretts.* She put the receiver back in its cradle and sat on the edge of the bed.

Buddy Briggs sat behind the steering wheel of his car in the Sterrett driveway. He wasn't ready for this meeting … this get-together … this confrontation … whatever it might turn into. He looked to his wife for consolation.

She smiled a sweet smile that said, "Everything is going to be all right." Then he looked in the rearview mirror at his daughter. She was staring back at him.

"Are you ready for this, Shirley Ann? Are you sure this is the way you want to do it?"

"Yes, Daddy, I am. I wish you were a little more in favor of it though."

"I'm doing my best here, honey."

"I know. You're saying all the right things but you still have an edge in your voice every time you talk to me. It was that way all through dinner."

Buddy wasn't sure how to respond to his daughter. Thankfully Amanda stepped in.

"Shirley Ann, I love you. We are tying hard to accept what you have done. And young lady, if an edge in your Daddy's voice is all you have to worry about, then you should consider yourself lucky. Now we are going to meet these folks and do the best we can. So don't demand more than we're able to give because we are doing just about all we can right now."

Buddy glanced at his wife, pleased and surprised. He loved her very much and wanted to tell her so. Instead he simply reached over and squeezed her knee. Then he turned off the engine and opened the car door to a gust of icy wind that showed no signs of abatement.

"Buddy! Amanda! Shirley Ann! Come in." The good doctor himself greeted them.

Mother and daughter entered, and Buddy fell behind and shook hands with the head of the household. Dr. Sterrett led them to the living room, took their coats, and offered them seats. Buddy and Amanda sat on the sofa and Shirley Ann sat next to them on an armless chair. Small talk about the weather filled in the spaces, but movement by the door caught Buddy's eye and when he looked up, he saw his future son-in-law standing there. Louis Wayne Sterrett stood straighter than most kids his age, and as he entered the room, he moved with the confidence of someone much older. His expression was equal parts solemnity and pleasantness. He maintained eye contact as he approached Buddy and shook his hand with a firmness that belied his youth. Despite all this, Buddy hated the very sight of him.

Doris Sterrett followed Louis Wayne into the room, all smiles and eyelids. It was obvious to Buddy she was, at best, medicated. He sort of wished he were too.

"I'm so glad all of you could come," Doris said, then fell into an overstuffed chair that matched the sofa. She sat with a dreamy smile and waited for her husband to take the lead.

"I won't try to pretend this isn't rather awkward for all of us," Dr. Sterrett said. "We have all had little time to adjust to this situation. But we're all here because the children requested this meeting. So there you are. And let me add that, as a medical professional, I am not inclined to accept this matter totally until a proper examination by an obstetrician is performed."

"By all means," added Doris.

"If that consultation proves what we all expect, then we will gladly welcome Shirley Ann and her child, our child, into our family. This is not how we would have planned it, of course, but life sometimes makes plans without asking our permission."

Buddy listened closely for something that might offend him so he could snap back at the self-centered "medical professional." But what was he going to do? Mix it up with him in his own living room two nights before Christmas? It wasn't the doctor's fault. And as much as it hurt to admit, it wasn't only the boy's fault either.

"Mr. Briggs, Mrs. Briggs, I have something I'd like to say," Louis Wayne began. "I can't tell you how sorry I am that this has happened. I'll take full responsibility. I know that doesn't change anything, but I don't want Shirley Ann to take the brunt of this. I know people will talk, but she and I don't care about that. We want to finish high school. Graduate in June if they'll let her finish. If not, she can go back next year. We've worked it all out. I can go to college close by and she can too, if she still wants to. We'll take turns taking care of the baby."

"You make it sound so shimple, honey, but it won't be that easy." Doris Sterrett's tongue belied the sober and respectful countenance she was straining to put forth.

"I know that, Mother, but we can do it."

Buddy spoke for the first time. "How much money can you make going to college, son? How much are they paying students nowadays?"

"I know what you're saying, sir, and I understand. But Pop was going to send me anyway. It won't be any more expense that it would have been and maybe even less if I go locally. Then I can get a part-time job and—well, we can make it work."

There was an odd silence in the room. The issue had been confronted and it seemed all who wanted to speak had had their say. Oh, there would be more to say in the future—some would need to wrestle with forgiveness, others with guilt, all would need to find a path to healing. But those were smaller conversations, private conversations.

Amanda broke the silence with her first words as she stood to leave.

"I want to wish the children the very best and offer our support in every way. They both have a lot of growing up to do and I think we all need to be here to help them however we can. We're soon going to welcome a very special little one into our lives and we can't let the importance of that escape us. God be with every one of us in this room. We're going to need him and each other."

Amanda's rallying speech said it all. It was the perfect cap to what could have been a difficult meeting. And if this had been the last thing Amanda said, all would have been well.

As they were putting their coats on and saying their goodnights, Amanda spoke to Doris, "I was so sorry to hear about your father. I know that kind of news is never easy—especially on top of all this."

"What newsh about my father?" Doris, though still slurring, was in wide-eyed control.

And Amanda was in wide-eyed shock. Could Doris be so far gone she didn't remember her father was dying? How could she explain herself? "His illness. I heard you received some bad news."

"Who told you that?"

Amanda was puzzled. "You told Rev. Franklin, didn't you?"

"Rev. Franklin doeshn't know anything about it. No one knows. Well, no one did until now." She turned and looked at Louis Wayne, who was staring at his mother.

"What's wrong with Granddad?"

Doris turned back to Amanda. "Colleen was going to call Rev. Franklin this afternoon but I stooped her … stopped her. We decided we didn't want anyone to know about our father's condition until after Christmas. Especishisly the children. Of course, now that has been ruined."

"I am so sorry, Doris. I had no idea. I thought everyone knew."

"Knew what?" Louis Wayne pressed for more information.

The look Doris gave Amanda needed no words but she said them anyway.

"Where did you hear this? Who told you this about my father?"

It was only hours ago. She couldn't lie and say she didn't remember. What could she say? The truth? Would the truth hurt? She didn't have time to think about this— Doris was waiting for an answer.

"Dove Franklin. I'm sure she heard it from her husband."

"Dove Franklin," Doris echoed. "She probably heard it from someone's husband, but not necessarily hers."

Dr. Sterrett took Amanda by the elbow and escorted them graciously to the door with all the good manners that Doris was lacking. They said their good nights. Dr. Sterrett kissed Shirley Ann on the cheek and wished each of them a Merry Christmas and stood in the doorway waving. As the Ford pulled away, he closed the door, rubbed his hand across his mouth and chin and turned to find his wife talking on the telephone.

"Little Miss Dovie Franklin has been spreading it around town that our father is on his death bed and where do you shuppose she heard it? You didn't call Rev. Franklin today after I told you not to did you? Hello. Colleen, are you lissning to me? Colleen, is Milton there? Put him on and I'll ask him myshelf?"

"Doris, are you drinking?"

CHAPTER

Mt. Jefferson was not a large town but it was more than a roadside attraction. It boasted near twenty-two thousand citizens according to the 1950 census and had enough stores to fulfill every need of those twenty-two thousand people. There were times it couldn't fulfill every wish, but every need— be it clothes, food, or shelter, church, social life, or new car—was seen to sufficiently. Mayor MacHaney summed it up best when he said Mt. Jefferson was big enough that when you walked down the street you wouldn't know everyone you met, but small enough that you couldn't walk down the street without seeing someone you knew. And though that folksy logic didn't keep him in office for a second term, he hit the nail dead center on the head.

Mt. Jefferson had department stores, grocery stores, dress shops, jewelers, haberdasheries, appliance stores, newsstands, theaters, and restaurants, ranging from cafes with checkered table cloths to lunch counters and ice cream and soda fountains too numerous to count. Auto supply stores, funeral parlors, hardware stores, and drug stores filled the side streets. You could get anything you needed in about eight blocks of easy walking. The streets were full twelve hours a day, six days a week, with happy shoppers, and Macalbee's sat right in the thick of it all.

But right now it was ten minutes after nine. Macalbee's was closed. The main floor was dark and empty of customers and clerks. The only light still on was one in the upstairs office, where Lois Pence was buttoning up her cloth coat while talking over her shoulder to Milton Sandridge.

"Do you want me to stay?"

"No. I'm just going to finish this row of figures and then I'm going, too."

"Mr. Sandridge, I don't mean to be personal, but I know it's been a hard day for you what with that Millie Franklin mess and the news you got about your father-in-law. If there is anything I can do ..."

"Thank you, Lois. But there's nothing."

"Give my regards to Mrs. Sandridge, and I'll see you in the morning."

"Good night, Lois."

The last noise he heard, besides the random cracking of the old wooden floors, was the back door opening and closing as Lois Pence went out onto the snow-covered sidewalk. He was finally alone. He tapped out a Chesterfield cigarette from the pack and struck a match. He loosened his tie and put his feet on his desk. Walter was on his mind. Their dinner together had been the highlight of his day, not that it would have taken much to highlight this particular day. They talked and laughed and shared a little downtown gossip and a couple of jokes, and Walter had been more open about his feelings than usual.

"Milton, what do you think of Dr. Sterrett? Tell me the truth. You've been in the family almost as long as he has."

"Why would you ask me such a question? But the truth is, I don't think much of him at all."

Both men threw back their heads and guffawed as if George Gobel had delivered the punch line.

"He's come over to the house a few times," Milton began, then leaned in and lowered his voice, "usually when Colleen or I are under the weather, but he never does anything. He always says it's not 'in his line' and he gives us a couple aspirins and tells us to call old Dr. Crone in the morning."

"There you go," Walter said as he threw his hands up in the air in mock disgust. "He's doing the same thing to me with this Dr. Yammie or whoever he is. I have never seen the man as much as carry a little black bag, and what kind of doctor are you if you don't have a little black bag for Pete's sake?"

They laughed again and went back to their meals and as Milton watched Walter eat the long-waited-for roast beef, he looked at his hands and his eyes and wondered about all the things Walter had seen and all the people he had known and all the feelings he had experienced. In that moment Milton thought of a million questions he wanted to ask Walter. But before Milton said a word, Walter asked, "What is it? What's on your mind, son?"

"What do you miss most about Ella?

"That's a hard one, boy. It's almost Christmas Eve. What're you doing asking questions like that?"

"You're not going to answer me are you?"

Ella had been the one true love of Walter's life. The faith she brought to their union had carried them through every uneven path that threatened their marriage. She had all the wisdom they needed and Walter had just enough wisdom to realize this.

She never let him stray and never let him regret it. She knew when to reel him in and when to give him more line. The sweetness of her memory lingered with him daily.

"Sure, I'll answer you. You know what I miss most? You probably think I'm going to say her cooking or her laugh or having her next to me when I go to sleep and when I wake up. Oh, I miss all that. You better believe I do. But you know what I miss most? And I miss it every day. Every sad day. Every day for the last five years. You know how a woman, and I'll bet Colleen does this too, goes through the house about dusk and turns lamps on in different rooms? Upstairs in the hall and in the bedroom. I used to fuss at her for wasting electricity, burning all those lamps when no one was in the room. But she ignored me and did it anyway. Men don't think to do little things like that when they're living by themselves.

Something as simple as turning a lamp on at dusk in different parts of the house makes the whole place warm and friendly. It makes a house a home. And to think I used to fuss at her for doing it."

There were tears in Walter's eyes, and Milton was sorry he put them there but he himself had been wondering what he would miss most if he no longer had Colleen. Some days he thought he wouldn't miss her at all. Some days he thought he'd miss her all the time. He tried to think of the one thing he'd miss the most, but it had taken Walter to put it in words. The warmth. That's what he'd miss.

As Milton sat in his office leaning back in his chair with his feet resting firmly on his daily report, he reached over and turned on the little radio Lois kept near the typewriter. Then he picked up the phone and dialed his home number. On the third ring Colleen answered.

"Hello."

"What are you doing?" he asked.

"I figured you'd be on your way home."

"Almost. Got a few more things here to do."

"Did you eat?"

"Yeah. I went to the hospital and ate with your dad."

"How is he tonight? I wanted to go back but he insisted I not go back out with the streets the way they are."

"Yeah, they're getting pretty bad," said Milton. "How are you really?"

"You know, hon, it just wasn't the shock for me that it was for Doris. I had a feeling there was something wrong from the day he went in and I've been preparing myself for it ever since. I didn't want to talk about it, but I was preparing myself inside. How about him? How is Dad doing?"

"He seemed better tonight than he has been since your mother died. He was full of himself. He was laughing and telling jokes. He was up and dressed when I got there and we went down to the cafeteria and we just had a great time together. Almost too good. I was afraid to leave, it was so good. Like I might never see him this full of life again. You know what I mean?"

"I know the feeling. I got some of that this evening too."

"How about Doris? Is she doing okay?"

"Depends on what you mean by 'okay.' She's drinking and taking tranquilizers and slurring every other word. Other than that I guess she's doing all right. By the way she called tonight. A rather strange thing happened."

"Yeah?"

"Well, I was going to tell you all this when you came home but do you want me to tell you now?"

"Sure, go ahead."

"Louis Wayne has gotten a girl in trouble. Maybe you already know this but if you don't, you'd better be sitting down. The girl is Shirley Ann Briggs, Buddy Briggs' daughter."

"I just saw Buddy this morning."

"Well, the whole Briggs family was over at Doris and Campbell's house tonight and they had a big pow-wow."

"What happened?"

"Everything was pretty calm best I could tell. I'll know more tomorrow when Doris is in better shape to talk."

"What are they going to do about it?"

"The two kids want to get married and have the baby and go to college and well, you know how kids are today. That kind of thing is not the scandal it was when we were sixteen and seventeen. One of these days there won't even be a thing called marriage. Girls will just deliver babies the way they have new furniture delivered. Some days, Milton, I'm *glad* we never had children."

There was an uncomfortable silence, but Milton had no words to fill it. He felt his headache return.

"And the other thing. After the Briggses left, Doris called me mad as a hornet and wanted to know how Amanda knew about Daddy's illness. Amanda said she heard it from Dove Franklin but I didn't call Paul because we had decided we wanted to keep it quiet till after Christmas. Milton, did you tell Dove?"

Every minute of this vexing, maddening day ran through his brain at breakneck speed. Did he tell Dove? Was he not supposed to? Did Dove tell Paul and Paul didn't know? Was this question a trap? Could there possibly be a right answer? His temples were throbbing.

"I ... don't know."

"You don't know? Have you seen her today?"

"Let me think. It's been one heck of day."

"You must have told her. Don't you remember if she was in the store or not?

"Oh, yes. Yes, she was. She was in the store."

"And you told her? What's wrong, Milton? You don't sound right. Are you okay?"

"I'm fine."

"You don't sound fine. Is there something you're not telling me?"

"Actually, yes, there is." Milton was beginning to recover. "I haven't told anyone, and I'd appreciate it if you'd keep it to yourself. This morning, about an hour after we opened, we caught Millie Franklin shoplifting."

"Oh, no! You aren't serious."

"Oh, I'm serious alright. I called Buddy and he took her home and then Dove came down here to see what had happened and then Paul came and it has been one big mess all day long."

"Well, why didn't you tell me this?"

"This is the first I've talked to you. And then the news about Walter came and that sort of knocked the wind out of me, and Dove was here just after that and I guess I probably said something to her. Why? Was I not supposed to?"

"No, that's all right, honey. You didn't know Doris

and I decided to keep it under wraps until after Christmas. You had no way of knowing."

"Well, I hope that wasn't a big problem."

"No, no. It will be fine. Are you about ready to come home?"

"What time is it?" He held up his arm and saw by the face of his Bulova that it was 9:35. "I'll be home by ten o'clock."

"I'll make you some tea. Bye-bye."

Milton placed the phone back in its cradle. His shirt was damp, his forehead was wet, and his heart was beating so hard he could see his tie jump as it lay against his chest. Millie Franklin's shoplifting, Dove Franklin's surprise appearance, Paul Franklin's visit by appointment, Walter's health news, the near slipup of who told whom, Louis Wayne and the Briggs girl, and Colleen's questioning on the phone just now … he didn't want many more days like this one. What he did want though was another cigarette.

Campbell Sterrett was coming down the stairs when he saw his son heading for the door.

"Where are you going this time of night?"

"I'm going to see granddad."

"You can't do that. Do you know what time it is? Visiting hours were over an hour ago."

"They'll let me go up."

"No, they won't. At eight-thirty they lock the front doors."

"Then I'll go in through the emergency room like you do."

"Son, sit down. It's been a rough day for all of us and I know how you feel, but going over there right now will only upset him. He needs his rest. Wait until tomorrow. The roads will be better and you both will have clearer heads about the matter."

"Pop, where's Louis Wayne going?"

"Nowhere, Hoyt."

"Why's he got his coat on?"

Louis Wayne's seven-year-old brother was in his pajamas with a dart gun in his hand. He knew nothing about what had happened in the Sterrett household today. He knew nothing about his future sister-in-law, the foreboding health of his grandfather, or why his mother had gone to bed at nine. His presence hampered Louis Wayne from putting up a further argument with their father, so Louis Wayne, like the good big brother he was, conceded by saying, "I'm going out to sweep off the driveway. Want to put on your boots and help?"

"Yeah!" Hoyt screeched and ran for the porch to get his coat and boots.

Louis Wayne would see his granddad tomorrow.

Lois Pence was in bed reading her *TV Guide* when the phone rang like a scream in a haunted house. She jumped out of bed and ran barefoot down the steps, more frightened with every ring. Every time the phone rang after ten o'clock, she panicked. By the time she lifted the receiver, she was almost too weak to expel a hello.

"Mrs. Pence? Is that you?"

"Yes, it is. Who is this?"

"This is Colleen Sandridge. Do you have any idea where Milton might be?"

"No, ma'am, I don't."

"Did you leave the store before he did?"

"Yes. I left shortly after nine and he was still at his desk. Is something wrong?"

"I'm not sure. I talked to him after you left I suppose. That was around nine thirty. He said he'd be home by ten and it's eleven now, and I was getting worried."

"Have you tried the store?"

"Three times. No one answers, so I'm sure he's gone. I thought maybe you might remember if he mentioned anything else he had to do."

"No, ma'am. Do you want me to go down to the store and check?"

"Not yet. Thank you. And I'm sorry to have called you so late. You were probably already in bed."

"That's okay, Mrs. Sandridge. I wasn't asleep."

"Well, good night."

"Good night."

CHAPTER

Walter was in his hospital room, in his hospital bed, with the lights out. Perhaps tomorrow he'd be back in his own house and his own bed. He'd have his own newspaper and his own radio and he could eat whatever he wanted, whenever he wanted. He might not even go to sleep. He might just sit up and read and watch Jack Paar. Then he remembered. Tomorrow night was Christmas Eve. Hospital days all ran together and, although he knew what the date was, it just hadn't hit him that Christmas was so near. But the way time flew for him anymore, Christmas was always just a few hours away. Except past Christmases. Those seemed like centuries ago and yet they flashed across his mind as vividly as the car lights from Rose Street flashed across the wall in front of him.

He looked through the open curtains at the flying snow. It could be anytime he wanted it to be. It could be now or it could be then.

Mt. Jefferson was a few years away from its first gasoline-powered ambulance. But even if the city had had one, because of the condition of the streets tonight it would have paled in comparison to the trusty old horse-drawn ambulance wagon the hospital sent to the Crown. Two hospital attendants crowded into the little dressing room. One carried a stretcher and the other one knelt down to speak to Adrienne.

"Ma'am, can you hear me?"

"Yes, I can hear you."

"Do you know where you were shot?"

"Ask Walter. I'm afraid to look."

"I have to ask you, ma'am. I want to know if you understand what has happened."

Adrienne repeated, in a fog, "Ask Walter."

The attendant refused to acknowledge that Walter was in the room, much less that he was both securing the wound and holding the hand of the wounded. He continued to talk to Adrienne.

"We're going to pick you up now and put you on a stretcher. If this hurts tell us." He looked back at his partner with the stretcher and said, "Let's go."

With this they pushed Walter out of the way, rolled Adrienne on the stretcher, and carried her out of the room, down the hall and out the stage door to the waiting wagon.

A crowd had gathered in the hallway and outside on the street. Walter stood with them and watched until the horses and passengers turned the corner and were out of sight. He was unaware of how long he had been standing there until a hand clasped his shoulder and he heard his father's voice say, "Let's go inside, son. They need to talk to you."

Walter followed his dad down the steps to the dressing room they had just left. Two men were waiting inside for them. He recognized one, the big beefy one with the red face, as Captain Bennington of the Mt. Jefferson police force. The other was much younger, smaller, and friendlier looking. Captain Bennington, who only a few months later would become the chief of police for a short term before leaving under some sort of scandal involving a local gambler and two waitresses, did all the talking.

"Walter, how are?" He didn't wait for Walter to answer. "You know me don't you, Walter? My name's Bennington. Your old man and me belong to the same lodge. I remember when you were born. And I want to help you, and I want you to help me. Do you understand?"

Walter looked at the two police officers, his father, and the pool of Adrienne's blood still in the middle of the floor.

"Walter, it looks like you're the only witness we have. Everybody else has skedaddled. So why don't you tell me exactly what happened here tonight."

Walter swallowed hard and said, "It was an accident," in hopes that was all he was going to have to say. But the night was young, and Captain Bennington had nowhere to go.

"How so, son?"

Walter wanted to remain loyal to Adrienne, but he didn't know how long he could hold out. Captain Bennington cut an intimidating figure.

"That's just it. It was an accident."

"Who shot her?"

"Does that matter?"

"Oh, yeah, boy. That matters. Cause if you don't tell me, I'm going to have to assume you did."

Walter turned anxiously and looked to his father for help. He got none. E. G. Selman was on the captain's side with this one.

"Just relax, Walter, and tell the captain what happened," his father said. "No one's blaming you for anything here. But you are the only one who knows what happened, and that young woman might not make it to tell her story. So it's all on you. Do it for her sake or somebody's going to get off scot-free."

His dad's words made sense. More sense than Adrienne's. Why did she want to protect the person who had done this to her? Nicholas and Simon were both guilty in a way. He did have an obligation and it was to Adrienne, not to Nicholas or Simon, no matter what she thought.

"From what I can piece together, Simon Croft was having a love affair with Adrienne. They sneaked around a lot down here behind her husband's back. Sometime this evening, before the performance, she and Simon must have had a spat and Simon hit her. He came to me to find a doctor and I couldn't, so instead I patched her up with makeup to get her through the show. All this time I thought it was her husband, Nicholas, who had hit her, but after the show, he came in and Simon was already in here, and when he saw her face marked up he went into a rage. Simon admitted he had done it and that's when Nicholas pulled out a gun and fired it. Adrienne got in the way. So it was an accident just like I said it was. Nicholas shot her but it was Simon's fault."

Captain Bennington looked a long time at Walter and let his words sink in before he spoke.

"The husband shot her but it was the boyfriend's fault. You have a cockeyed way of looking at things, young man. What part did you play in all this? What were you doing down here when the shot was fired?"

"I came down to see if she was all right after the show."

"She just let you in her dressing room? A boy like you? Just let you walk in?"

"Yes, sir. We had become friends."

"I believe you had, Walter. I believe you had. So you and this Simon Craft, Croft, were sitting in the dressing room of another man's wife and her husband comes in. What did he think of that? What did Nicholas think?"

"I guess it made him pretty mad. He never really said. When he came in, he noticed the bruise on her face and that made him mad. He wanted to know who did that to her."

"Did you tell him who did it?"

"No, sir. I didn't know at the time. Not until Simon started crying."

"And then what did Nicholas have to say?"

"He didn't say anything. He just pulled the gun out of his pocket and pointed it at Simon and shot."

"Is this the gun?"

"Yes, sir."

"One shot?"

"Yes, sir."

"Now this is a real important part, Walter. I want you to think real hard and remember exactly, I mean exactly what happened next. When did these men leave the room?"

"Right after he shot her."

"Right after? Immediately after? They just took off running?

"Well, Nicholas went first. Then Simon."

"Neither one looked after the lady?"

"I ran to get my dad and he came in and told me to stay with her while he went for help."

"Your dad left you in the room with two men, one of them a possible murderer?"

"I can answer that, Captain." E. G. interrupted the interrogation. "I put Walter in charge of the girl because I didn't know which one of the men had fired. I picked up the pistol before I left and put it in my pocket so I knew there was no further danger. But on the side of caution I instructed two stagehands to stand at the door. I know both of those men and I knew they could handle any trouble an actor could give them with or without a pearl-handled pistol."

"Fine, fine … but I want Walter to tell his story first." Captain Bennington was irritated that the elder Selman had broken his rhythm. He continued to address his questions to Walter. "You were the only one in there when they left?"

"Me and Adrienne."

"Of course. Did you help them escape?"

"Me? No, sir. I never took my hand off her wound."

"Walter, someone in the hall heard you say," and he went to his notes for the proper quote, "'*Get out of town before the police come. You, too, Simon.*' Then they heard you yell '*Simon, run. Get out of here.*' Is that right, Walter?"

"I was just repeating what Adrienne told me to say."

"I see."

Walter's throat was frozen. Nothing was sounding right in the retelling. Bennington leaned back with his topcoat open and his silver watch chain shining, and Walter felt as if he was beating him over the head with his own words. He could no longer think straight. He just wanted it to be over. He just wanted to go up the hill to the hospital and see if Adrienne was going to be okay.

"That's all we'll need you for tonight, Walter. But if those two dandies aren't in our net by morning, we may need to talk to you again."

Lenity General had been modernized and updated with each decade, but this was the very same building where Adrienne had been taken all those years ago. The very same hospital Walter had walked to that night to sit in the waiting room until dawn, awaiting news from the second-floor operating room. That news finally came just as his own news had come today.

Walter fell asleep. He was too tired to dream anymore.

CHAPTER

Buddy Briggs was used to getting phone calls in the middle of the night. It came with the job. But familiarity didn't change the nature of the calls. He, like Lois Pence, knew that a telephone ringing in a darkened room was usually the harbinger of bad news. He knew as he picked up the phone this was something that would require him to get out of his warm bed and head into the snowy night, which only looked pretty from inside a cozy room.

"Yes?"

"Buddy?"

"Speaking."

"This is Colleen Sandridge. I'm sorry to call you at this hour. But I'm worried about Milton. It's eleven thirty, and he still isn't home."

Buddy propped himself up on his elbow and turned on the bedside lamp.

"Is he always home by this time?"

"Oh, most definitely. I just talked to him two hours ago and he said he was coming right home."

"Where was he then?"

"At the store."

"Has he ever stopped off at someplace to get a drink or a sandwich?"

"Never that I know of. I told him I was going to make him some tea. That was around nine thirty and he said he would be home by ten. I've called his assistant manager...."

"Lois?"

"Yes, Lois Pence, and she said he was at his desk when she left."

"And what time was that?"

"Shortly after nine. I don't want to sound like an alarm-ist but this has never happened before, and I don't know what to do. I'm sorry I woke you up but I didn't know who else to call."

"That's okay. Listen, let me do a little checking and I'll call you right back. Okay?"

"Thank you so much, Buddy."

Buddy sat up on the edge of the bed and rubbed both hands across his eyes. He looked to see if the phone or the conversation had wakened Amanda. Her eyes were closed, but she asked, "Who was that?"

"Colleen Sandridge. She can't find Milton."

Amanda never said a word and never opened her eyes. Thoughts raced through her head that she couldn't tell her husband. She was a faithful wife but she was also a loyal friend, and she hadn't told Buddy the things Dove confided in her. Suddenly all those things, all those out-of-the-way meeting places and out-of-town day trips only she knew about, caused her imagination to explode. She might be able to solve this for Buddy. She could start by calling to see if Dove was home. But when she rolled over and looked at the clock and saw it was only twenty-five minutes until midnight, she scrapped that plan immediately. If Dove was there or if she wasn't, what reason could she possibly give for calling? She closed her eyes again and lay there with her thoughts. The only thing she could think to do was pray, and she wasn't sure quite how to pray about this situation.

Buddy was in the kitchen on the phone.

"Mt. Jefferson Police Department."

"Lorrie, this is Briggs. Who's got patrol duty down-town tonight?"

"That would be Officer Tolley."

"Have him check on the parking lot behind Macalbee's to see if a green '56 Chevy is there. Two-door."

"License number?"

"I have no idea. Just have him check and call me at home as quick as you can."

"Will do, Lieutenant."

Amanda walked in the kitchen as Buddy was attempting to make a pot of coffee. She had considered staying in bed but couldn't justify inaction while hearing her husband banging around in the kitchen looking for a sugar bowl that had sat on the same shelf for the past eight years. She smiled at him and said, "Sit down. I'll fix it." A moment later she asked, "Where do you think he might be?"

"Beats me. Milton seldom drinks. There's not much open anyway this time of night and especially on a night like this. I'm a little worried he might have slipped off the road somewhere. I was just trying to figure how many different ways he could have driven home. We'll backtrack him that way and then if that doesn't turn up anything …"

"What then?"

"I don't know. We'll see."

The phone rang again. Buddy answered on the first ring.

"Lieutenant? Officer Tolley just radioed in. That car, green '56 Chevy, is on the lot, covered with snow."

"Thanks, Lorrie. Tell Tolley to meet me there in fifteen minutes."

"On the lot?"

"On the lot. And, Lorrie, call Lois Pence. I don't know the number or the address. Tell her we need the key to the store. She's the assistant manager. Send Tolley over to her house to get it."

"What if she won't give him the key? You know how finicky some of these merchants are."

"Then have Tolley bring her along with the key." Buddy held the phone for a second before hanging it up. He looked at Amanda with a puzzled look.

"What?" she asked out of frustration.

"His car is still at the store. It hasn't been moved. That means he's still inside or left with someone else. Or someone is in the store with him."

Amanda felt her breathing become irregular and was sure her color had drained. She was overcome with the feeling that if she withheld what she knew from her husband it would be as if she was being unfaithful. Where was her loyalty? To her husband, of course. She had already betrayed Dove once with that gaffe about Walter Selman. But she couldn't let Buddy walk into such a sticky situation blind. Or maybe he already knew? Maybe he was thinking the same things.

Buddy was back in the bedroom dressing hurriedly in a pair of khakis and a crew neck sweater. He came through the kitchen putting his arm into his overcoat.

"Buddy, I have to tell you something"

"Can't it wait, honey? I sort of have my hands full right now."

"No, it can't. It's about this situation."

"About this? About Milton?" Her words had stopped him cold.

"Yes. Oh, I don't know how to tell you this. Promise

me, Buddy, what I am about to say will never leave this room. Please promise you'll never tell a soul."

"What's up, Amanda?" It was one of the few times she'd detected the policeman in his voice when addressing her. He looked her directly in the eye and held the stare until she spoke.

"I might know what's going on with Milton. I might. I don't know for sure. But you think he might have someone in the store with him, and if he does, I might know who it is."

"Go on." The policeman was gone. She was talking to Buddy again and that made it a little bit easier. But only a little bit.

"Dove Franklin and Buddy are old friends from years ago in Richmond."

"I know that."

"I mean real good friends, Buddy. And they see each other whenever they can. They sneak around and they swear nothing really bad happens but they still sneak around. And I'm the only one that knows about it."

"How do *you* know about it?"

"Dove told me. If anyone is in that store, in that

office with him tonight, I just know it's her. I don't want a bunch of policemen barging in there. This mess would be all over Main Street before Christmas morning. Please don't hate me for keeping this from you. I was just trying to be a good friend to Dove. I've wanted to tell you so many times but I just didn't know what to do."

"Not your fault. I'll just make sure I go in first. I'll leave Tolley at the door."

This news left Buddy numb, but with a lot of questions. Questions he didn't have time to ask. It also left him relieved, because when Amanda began to tell him, a fear from down inside crept up in his stomach that she was going to reveal something about herself.

The phone rang and made them both jump.

"Yes."

"Buddy, this is Colleen."

"I was just getting ready to call you, Colleen," Buddy lied. He had no intention of calling Colleen until he had found Milton. He looked at Amanda, who was sitting at the table with her head buried in her hands. "We're going to check a few places out and then I'll get back to you."

"That's what I'm calling you about. I've been out riding around looking for him since we talked. And I found his car. It's still on the lot behind the store."

Buddy's face muscles tightened. "What? Where are you now?"

"I'm at that phone booth in front of the Jefferson Bank. I can see the back door of the store from here but I don't have a key, of course. I banged on the door a few times but I don't know if he's in there."

"Colleen, you need to go home and let me handle this. Will you do that?"

"I need to get in the store. It's freezing out here. Can you get a key?"

"Colleen, go home."

"I'll wait here till you get a key. Certainly the police know how to get in a locked door."

"Colleen—" but the rest of that sentence was lost to the dial tone from the other end of the line. Buddy slammed the phone down a little harder than he meant. It startled Amanda, who looked up with tears in her eyes. Shirley Ann was standing in the doorway in her pajamas.

"Mama. Daddy. What's going on?"

"Your daddy has been called out tonight, that's all."

"Then why are you crying?"

Amanda sighed heavily. "It's just life, Shirley Ann, life. Go back to bed."

CHAPTER

Buddy met Milton shortly after the war in the spring of
'47. He had only been in town for a month or so when
Milton called the police station about a theft problem
at Macalbee's. Buddy, a uniformed officer at the time,
answered the call. Buddy remembered feeling like he was
being watched as he walked in the store's front door and
down the aisles. He stopped in the middle of the store
and looked all around and then finally spotted Milton
standing by the window in his office. Milton waved Buddy
up, and when he got to the office, Milton was waiting
with coffee and a handshake."

"How you doing? I'm Milton Sandridge."

"Buddy Briggs."

"Sit down."

"Thank you. That's a pretty neat window you got there," Buddy said. "You've got a bird's-eye view of everything."

"Well, not everything or I wouldn't have needed to call you."

They both laughed.

"I can look out this window and see shoplifters and window shoppers and serious shoppers. I see people who just come in to get out of the cold or the heat, kids who just want to finger everything and don't have a dime to spend, and comparison shoppers from other stores. I see people who come in each week to pay down their layaways and those who show up once and never return. And I see clerks loafing and gossiping and trying to look busy. But what I don't see, Officer ... what was it?"

"Briggs. Buddy."

"What I don't see, Buddy, is whoever it is that's stealing me blind."

Choosing to call him Buddy that first day sealed their friendship.

Buddy drank another cup of coffee while Milton laid out his problem.

"We've got merchandise missing. And some of it is big stuff. We keep a rack of winter coats there toward the back. Last week we lost four, all different sizes. Last Friday an entire bolt of cloth came up missing. My assistant and I pretty much keep watch on the store throughout the day. Not every minute, mind you, but we keep an eye on things. I know we'll miss shoplifters who take small stuff. Thread and scissors and stockings and socks and things they can stuff in their pockets. But this big stuff has me stumped. One day last week a tricycle was missing. Now tell me how somebody gets a tricycle out the front door without somebody seeing them?"

Buddy thought for a moment and offered a plan.

"Give me a week. Don't do anything until you hear back from me. And don't tell anyone why I was here this morning. Let's just keep this between the two of us."

Milton agreed, and after they talked a few minutes more about the problems of downtown parking, the weather, and the Yankees, Buddy stood up, shook hands, and left. About halfway through the store, he turned and looked up and waved. Milton waved back. Buddy knew he'd be watching.

That evening at closing time Buddy changed into his street clothes and walked down the narrow alley between Macalbee's and the neighboring store. He checked all the windows and found everything to be in order. The next evening, he did the same thing and found things to be in order. On Friday he went home, ate supper, and came back at ten minutes after seven and repeated his alley trek. The third window he tried was unlocked. He raised it, looked inside to a dark basement and closed it again gently. He went back to the station and called the Macalbee's number. Milton answered from his office.

"Hello."

"Milton?"

"This is he."

"Buddy Briggs here. Are you alone?"

"Yeah, I'm alone."

"I think I've got a lead on your burglar."

"Burglar? Do we have a burglar?"

"You might. Are you getting ready to leave soon?"

"Just ready to walk out the door."

"It'll be another hour before it gets good and dark, so go on home. Don't change a thing. Meet me back here in about thirty minutes. Park by the station. I'll be watching for you."

"What are we doing exactly?"

"We're catching bad guys. I'll see you in about thirty."

Thirty minutes later Milton pulled up behind the police station and parked his car. Buddy was waiting for him. Together they walked through the alley to the back of Macalbee's.

"I think I've found *how* your merchandise is leaving the store but I wanted you here when we found out *who* it was leaving with."

They hid behind a service truck and settled in for a long wait. But they made good use of their time. They smoked half a pack of Lucky Strikes and talked about everything from women and Harry Truman to Jackie Robinson and Groucho Marx. They agreed on three out of the four.

Milton was about to argue that Groucho used to be funnier with his brothers when Buddy laid a hand on his arm to silence him. A figure came around the back corner of the store and was creeping slowly toward them. They both watched as the shadow crept to the third window and raised it as high as it would go. The perpetrator took out a flashlight and shined it inside as he climbed down into the store basement. Then the stock started flying out the window. First a couple of sweaters, then a crate of candy, a scooter, and finally, two sets of bed sheets and pillowcases. When the burglar stuck his leg through the window to make his escape, Buddy made his move. As the thief reached up to pull down the window sash, Officer Briggs cuffed him.

Milton saw it all at close range. The heist. The arrest. And the fear in the eyes of Earl Meeks, his assistant manager, as Buddy walked him across the adjoining alley to the police station. From that day on he had vowed never to allow the home office to send him an out-of-town assistant. He demanded to hire his own and that's how Lois Pence got her job.

The roads were worse than Buddy had expected. If Milton *was* out in this mess in someone else's car, he might just be in a ditch or over the side of a hill. And what about his wife? Colleen had been risking her life on the roads too. What was he going to do with her when he got to the store? If she was still in the phone booth or even sitting on the parking lot, she couldn't miss them. Maybe he could plead police business and danger. He didn't know her very well so he didn't know how easily she could be bluffed. He would just have to be fast on his feet.

As the headlights from his cruiser flooded across the back of Macalbee's and came to a stop, he saw the three of them walking up to the back door: Officer Tolley, Colleen Sandridge, and Lois Pence.

Tolley walked to the car as soon as it came to a stop and left the women standing under a small overhang just outside ear range.

"Lieutenant, I had to bring the woman with me. She wouldn't give up the key. She's a feisty one."

"What about the wife? What kind of shape is she in?"

"She's pretty upset. Not crying or anything, but concerned and determined. I can't tell if she's mad or worried. She just seems a little out of it. What's going on exactly? What are we doing here and what are we looking for?"

"Her husband didn't come home tonight. He may be inside and he may not be."

"This guy a friend of yours"?

"Yeah. And Tolley, it's a little sticky. I'm going to need you to keep these women just inside once we get in the building. I want to search the premises by myself."

"You got 'Henry' with you?"

"Church is the only place I go without him."

Colleen and Lois were women from two different worlds. Lois was a widow devoted to her job, and Colleen was a wife devoted to her husband. Milton was their one and only bond. Before tonight their past conversations had amounted to "Hello. How are you today? Is Milton there?"

"You look nearly frozen, Mrs. Sandridge," Lois said.

"I'm all right. I wish they would hurry up though. Do you have the key?"

"Yes, I do. That officer wanted me to give it to him but I wouldn't do it. I told him I didn't care if he was J. Edgar Hoover, I wasn't giving it to him so he said 'Get your coat,' and here I am."

"I think you should go ahead and open it so we can step inside where it's warm."

Lois Pence was digging in her purse for the key when the lieutenant walked toward them. Buddy still didn't know exactly how he was going to play this.

"Colleen. Lois," he began. "Before we open that door, here's what I want you to do. After you turn on the lights, I need both of you stay by the door with Officer Tolley. Okay?"

Lois spoke as she was turning the key. "That's fine with me. Here, I'll flip the switches."

As the light began to fill the building, Colleen pushed past Lois and headed in a near run toward Milton's office. Buddy followed behind. He called for her and pleaded with her to stop but she ignored him. Just as she opened the door to the stairs that led to the office, Buddy caught up to her and grabbed her arm. Somehow she pulled away and started running up the narrow staircase. He heard noise coming from behind the office door. The radio. And as Colleen flung the door open and the music became louder, they froze in horror. Milton was slumped over his desk.

Colleen screamed. Buddy grabbed her by the shoulders and moved her out of the doorway and went behind the desk. He put his finger against Milton's neck, feeling for a pulse. When he looked up, Lois Pence and Officer Tolley were in the room and Colleen was in a chair with her hands to her mouth. Buddy looked at Tolley.

"Radio for an ambulance."

"Is he alive?" Lois asked. Buddy was surprised by her calmness.

"Yes."

Officer Tolley stepped out into the small hallway, and with much crackling and code, called for help. Lois put her arm around Colleen's shoulders and said soft and comforting things that no one else could or needed to hear. Buddy stood by the desk looking at his friend. He was suddenly aware that the only sound in the room besides Colleen's sobbing was Perry Como singing "It's Beginning to Look a Lot like Christmas." He reached over and turned the radio off.

CHAPTER

Sleep did not come easy for Walter. He was in and out of consciousness and awake every half hour. The shadows on the wall were more intrusive than the soft sounds from the hall. His waking thoughts and his dreams were intermingling. Sometimes he was aware of a nurse being in the room. Sometimes he thought it was his dad. Sometimes he thought it was Captain Bennington. Once, he was sure it was Adrienne.

Young Walter stayed in the hospital lobby all night. He fell asleep in an armless chair twisted unnaturally in a position only a sixteen-year-old could survive. When he awoke with the first light of morning shining across him and onto the patterned carpet at his feet, he saw his mother and his father sitting opposite him, watching his every squirm and twitch. They had no way of knowing what the police's next step would be and neither did they know beyond all doubt why their son was involved in the first place.

His mother spoke first. "Son, are you ready to come home and eat some breakfast?"

Walter ignored her question. "What's happened? Have you heard anything from upstairs?"

His father answered. "They operated in the night. I talked to the doctor just a couple of hours ago."

"Is she going to be all right?"

"That's hard to say, Walter. She's in pretty bad shape."

"I want to see her."

"I don't think that's such a good idea, son," his mother said. "I don't think it would be proper and I don't think it would be allowed."

"Who's the doctor?"

"Dr. Larnette. He's been with her all night. He's the same doctor, you might remember, that looked after your aunt when she ..."

E. G. Selman's sentence was interrupted by the appearance of the until-now silent policeman who had accompanied Captain Bennington at the theater the night before. He walked up, said good morning, and then looked to Walter. "She's awake and she's asking to see you."

Walter followed the policeman down the hallway to the stairs, and at Mrs. Selman's insistence, E. G. trailed behind. At the top of the staircase Captain Bennington took over from his subordinate and escorted them to the room. The hall was dark and quiet, and a uniformed officer was sitting in a chair outside. He rose as the three of them approached. Dr. Caywood Larnette exited room 226, surveyed the group, and spoke to them jointly, quietly, and with authority.

"Mrs. Knoles is in a very serious way. The bullet pierced her intestines in sixteen places and perforated her bladder. We've done all we can to prevent infection and make her comfortable. She is conscious. Thankfully she's been in very little pain with all this." Dr. Larnette rubbed his hand across his bald head and breathed deeply, settling his gaze solidly on Walter. "And, young fellow, if you're Walter, she's asking to see you and no one else."

Bennington stepped forward. "She'll see him, Doc, but I need to be in there with whoever she's talking to."

"Oh, for goodness sake, Calvin," said Walter's dad. "Let the woman be. If she wants to talk to the boy, let her be."

Walter had never heard his dad talk to Captain Bennington this way and had certainly never heard him use his given name. Apparently Walter wasn't the only one surprised by this outburst because it stopped the captain cold.

"Well, I don't want them in there cooking up some kind of story. He can go in, but I'm standing right here till he comes out."

Dr. Larnette stepped aside and opened the door for Walter, who entered slowly and anxiously. The bed near the far wall consumed the small body in pristine sheets. He moved forward and stood as close as he dared and kept his silence until he saw the slight movement of head and eyes.

"Walter, you're here."

"Yes. How are you?" He knew how silly this question was as soon as it hit the air, but it was as much sense as his nerves would allow.

"Come closer. I don't want them to hear me outside."

Walter inched toward the bed until his leg was touching it. Adrienne reached for his hand and pulled him gently until his head was bent near her lips.

"What did you tell them, Walter? Did you tell them it was an accident? That Nick wasn't to blame?"

"Yes."

"Have you seen Nick?"

"No."

"You must find him. Please, Walter."

"How?"

"You'll find a way. You'll find a way. Go on now and tell them outside that I just wanted to thank you for your kindness. Don't tell them we talked of Nick. Do you understand? And tell Nick I'm going to be just fine."

With this her head rolled back facing the wall and Walter was left standing in the semi-darkness more confused than when he had entered. He walked to the door. The doctor pushed past him and went back in the room to see to Adrienne. Bennington glared down at him with steely eyes.

"What did she want?"

"She just wanted to thank me."

"Thank you? Thank you for what?"

"For being her friend," and Walter walked back to the staircase and down the steps. E. G. followed at a distance and Captain Bennington just stood there with a puzzled look on his face.

The last murder Bennington had worked was right after the turn of the century in the summer of 1900, when Daniel Moss had been found dead on the back porch of John Tuttlemeyer's farmhouse. The cause of death was a shotgun blast to the face. It was a clear case of breaking and entering and self-defense—the whole town knew the Moss boys were nothing but trouble. An investigation was conducted, but charges were never brought. Of course, this wasn't a murder case … yet. Bennington knew there was a slim chance the actress would survive … but he wasn't optimistic about it. It would become a murder case, he thought. Eventually.

By ten the next morning Walter was back in the theater doing what he always did the morning after a show. He was cleaning the aisles and sweeping out between the rows of seats. There would be no show tonight. His father told him that within one hour of the ambulance carrying Adrienne off to the hospital, most of the remaining cast and crew had packed up and left town. The local police had done a poor job of securing the room as a crime scene, and when they returned to comb through any possible evidence, it had all disappeared. Someone had even mopped up the blood. Walter's dad said it was an old circus troupe tactic of leaving no trace behind that could convict one of their own, even if one of their own was guilty. Did Nicholas and Simon leave with them? And where were they? In a neighboring town? On the way back to Baltimore? Adrienne had asked him the impossible when she asked him to find Nick.

Walter was filling the trash cans outside the theater when he was suddenly aware that someone was watching him from the curb. It was a small boy, maybe seven years old, in a filthy coat much too small for him and much too light for the bitingly cold weather. He had no gloves and his nose was red and running, but his eyes were alert and watching Walter's every move. Walter continued his cleanup, picking up debris off the sidewalk, and every time he looked back, the dirty-faced little boy was still staring at him. Finally he came closer and asked, "Are you Walter?"

"Yeah."

"Here." The boy handed Walter a folded note and then ran away as if Satan himself was on his tail.

Walter watched until he rounded the corner and disappeared. Then he unfolded the note and with great difficulty read the scrawling on the paper. *Am in hiding near train depot. Come past tracks at dark. Need to talk. Bring no one. Nick.*

Walter spent the rest of the day at the hospital. As he sat in the lobby, he saw flowers being delivered every half hour—big beautiful Christmas wreaths and colorful poinsettias. Later he would learn that Adrienne had received everything from nuts and fruit to bedclothes and cosmetics, gifts from the good people of Mt. Jefferson to the ailing, and maybe dying, Adrienne, whom they had only known and admired for one performance. It was obvious to everyone, through the newspaper and by word of mouth, that Adrienne was without any formal family. Mt. Jefferson, in an expression of communal kindness, had adopted her.

By suppertime small groups of citizens had gathered

in the cold outside the front of Lenity General, showing support and awaiting news. The evening was beginning to pale into darkness when Walter weaved his way through the small groups of well-wishers along the front steps and set his sights on the train depot, about six blocks away.

Walter crossed the tracks and stood for a few moments in hopes that someone would come to him. Time passed and no one came. He started walking along the tracks in ever-increasing darkness and cold. About a half-mile from the depot, he could smell food cooking. He looked to his left over a shallow embankment and saw small flickers of flame coming from what appeared to be a company of individual campfires. The secluded field could only be seen from the train or the tracks. His eyes were adjusting to the sight and the lack of light when a voice he had heard before spoke his name.

"Walter."

He jumped and turned and saw the dirty little boy who had delivered the note. The boy then ran down the embankment and toward the camp. Walter waited. A larger figure left the camp and started up the hill toward him. Nicholas Knoles. There was no greeting. No "thank you" for coming. Nicholas went straight to the business at hand.

"How is she?"

"Pretty bad."

"Is she going to live?"

"I don't know."

"I didn't mean to shoot her. She knows that doesn't she?"

"Yes, sir."

Walter was mesmerized by Nicholas' appearance. He was still wearing his expensive street clothes and long heavy coat, but he looked as if he had not slept in the past twenty-four hours. His tired eyes stared at Walter with a cry for help, and Walter, who had both feared and felt sorry for this man in the past day and a half, sensed genuine remorse in him.

"Can you get a message to her?"

"Maybe. They're watching her pretty close."

"Tell her I'm here. Tell her I haven't left. Tell her I'm sorry and I love her. Will you do that?"

"If I can." Walter looked past him down the hillside into the camp. "Who are all those people? Is that the cast and crew?"

"No. That's just some hobo camp that took me in. I can stay here with them until something happens or they get run off."

Walter had never seen anything like it before and found himself staring at the strange but rather pretty sight of the small campfires against the oncoming night.

"And, Walter, one more thing."

"Yes, sir."

"Do you have any money?"

Startled at the request, he dug into his pockets and pulled out all he had.

"Eighty-five cents."

"That'll help." Nicholas Knoles, star of stages throughout America and Europe, reached out his hand and snatched it from the boy. "That'll help."

The gifts and letters and telegrams and notes of well-wishing continued to pour into the hospital until a special committee from the Ladies Auxiliary of Local Affairs volunteered to intercept them and manage the barrage of kindness. On the ground floor of the Faith Presbyterian Church, the largest in the city, they began to keep account of all the gifts and cards that Mt. Jefferson's most famous visitor was generating. The church also became an information post on her medical status to help keep the corridors and front steps of the hospital clear. On her third night of hospitalization and exactly one week before Christmas Day, a community choir from all the neighboring churches gathered on the lawn under her window and sang carols. It was uplifting, depressing, thoughtful, and eerie all at the same time. Walter found himself either in the lobby or with the crowd every waking minute. He adroitly avoided being seen by Captain Bennington and was secretly trying to spot Dr. Larnette, who never seemed to come out of the building. It wasn't until Monday evening just before the choir began to sing again that he saw the doctor getting out of his Oldsmobile runabout. Walter met him coming up the walkway.

"Dr. Larnette, can I talk to you for just a minute?"

Larnette stopped and looked at the boy and answered him with an upward toss of his head and the raising of his eyebrows.

"Sir, I'm the one who came up to see Adrienne, ah, Mrs. Knoles the other morning. Can I see her again, please?"

"She's not in much shape to have visitors, and anyway you'd have to clear that with the police. Captain Bennington."

"He'll never let me, sir. You're the only one who can get me up there, and I really need to see her."

"Why, boy? Why do you need to see her?"

Walter weighed quickly whether or not he could trust the truth with this stone-faced doctor. He didn't know the right thing to do, but he knew he had to take a chance for Adrienne's sake. When he started talking, he was not sure what his next word was going to be.

"Captain Bennington doesn't like me. He thinks I'm not telling him the truth about the shooting, but I am. Adrienne has nobody here to talk to. I'm her only friend. I really just need a couple of seconds just to let her know that I'm still here. I think it would mean a lot to her."

Dr. Larnette squinted at the boy and the expression on his face said he knew he was being handled but he thought it was for a good reason.

"You come to the door in the back at six o'clock and be careful."

"Yes, sir, and thank you."

Walter was waiting in the shadows when the back door to the hospital opened and Dr. Larnette motioned him in.

They went silently up the back stairs and down the hall to Adrienne's room. When Walter had cleared the doorway, the doctor closed the door behind him without ever saying a word and disappeared down the hall.

"Walter?"

"Yes, ma'am."

"Did you find him?"

"Well, actually he found me, but yes, we talked."

"And?"

"He's staying in a hobo camp by the rails just outside of town. He said to tell you he was sorry and that he wasn't leaving."

"Walter, is it nice outside?"

"Nice? It's very cold. There's still snow and ice on the ground."

"I wish it was spring. I love flowers, Walter. What's your favorite flower?"

"I don't know."

"I love roses. Are there any roses out there? Oh, but you said snow and ice. I guess there couldn't be roses. Am I making any sense, Walter? I can't tell."

"You're doing just fine."

"Did he say anything else?"

"I beg your pardon?"

"Nick. Did he say anything else?"

"Well, yes. He said to tell you he loves you."

Walter wasn't sure she heard this last sentence because her eyes were closed. She had fallen back to sleep, giving into the haze of narcotics she had been constantly plied with these past few days. Her breathing was easy and Walter hoped the same for her pain.

He touched her hand before he left.

CHAPTER

Colleen rode in the back of the ambulance with Milton. She thought he squeezed her hand at one point. While one attendant worked on Milton, the other had his hands full keeping the emergency vehicle on the ice-covered streets. Colleen kept talking to her husband through it all, even though she had no idea what she was saying. Her mind was other places and on other times. She recalled the first time she'd met him. A summer dance at the pavilion in the park. It was June and he had on a white shirt with his sleeves rolled up. The tie he had removed was hanging over his rearview mirror. His hair was long and he was chewing Cloves chewing gum.

Funny the things you remember when you begin fearing that memories may be all you have left.

Her girlfriend, Betty Jean Fauber, had introduced them, and they danced and talked for hours and he talked her into letting him take her home that first night. She refused as long as she could without offending him and finally allowed him to take her to Betty Jean's house. This way Betty Jean could take her home later and she'd never have to explain to her parents why she got in the car with a man she had only known for a few hours. But hours was all it took. She was in love before she went to sleep that night. A couple of days later when her parents met him, they were just as taken as she. The only one in the family who wasn't so easily impressed was her sister. Doris never liked Milton and never pretended to. They spoke and were pleasant to one another, but it ended there. Doris didn't think he was good enough to be in the family. But, as their daddy had once said, given the chance, Doris could have found fault with John the Baptist.

Then her mind jumped to Milton and her dad playing golf together on Wednesday afternoons. She saw visions of him serving Communion at church on Sunday mornings. She saw him in his annual Santa suit at the store. In his softball uniform. In his first pair of Bermuda shorts.

In a tuxedo at his cousin's wedding. In that white shirt with his sleeves rolled up. She could smell the shaving lotion he wore that night. She squeezed his hand and said a prayer and the attendant looked over at her and, thank God, smiled.

When they arrived at the emergency room, Buddy and Lois Pence and the other policeman were waiting for them. Milton was whisked down a hallway and into a room and out of Colleen's sight. Buddy took her by the arm and they all sat in the waiting room. There were only five other people in the room—an elderly woman in a tattered coat and tears being consoled by an apparent daughter and son-in-law, and a young mother walking a crying baby back and forth past the large frosted window, talking to her, trying to quiet her constant wailing. Colleen's nerves, already near an edge, became more upset at these scenes and sights. Lois was Colleen's surprising rock and comforter. Officer Tolley stood by the automatic sliding entranceway, and Buddy sat in a chair opposite her.

"Buddy, did you call my sister?"

"I talked to her husband. He said they would be right over."

As the door slid open, the doctor and his wife came in and went straight to Colleen. Doris kneeled in front of her and spoke in soft tones while Campbell Sterrett greeted Buddy and Lois.

"Have you heard anything?" the doctor asked.

"No."

"I'll see what I can find out."

"Thanks." Buddy sat back and waited. He hadn't expected to see these people again tonight. He wanted to call Amanda and let her know what was going on but he didn't want to leave Colleen just yet, even though her sister was here with her. For some reason he felt even more uneasy since she arrived. Doris looked in worse shape than Colleen. He only knew Doris from church and never had much contact with her before tonight except for one occasion when a patrolman brought her into the station, threatening arrest.

He had been at his typewriter doing some late work when he heard a commotion at the front desk. He looked up and saw Officer Charles Banes leading a woman in by the arm who was yelling in his face. The thing Buddy remembered most about her rantings were the two sentences she kept repeating over and over, "Take your hands off me," and "Do you know who I am?" A second look told Buddy he did know who she was and he walked out into the front desk area and asked what was going on.

"She was driving without a license," Officer Banes quickly explained.

"I have a license. I just don't have it with me."

"That's the point of having one. You got to have it with you," Banes said, while still holding on to her upper arm.

"Take your hands off me and let me call my husband. He'll bring it down here and settle this whole thing."

Banes didn't give up easily. "He can bring it down here but that still don't change the fact that you were driving without it."

Buddy stepped in to give some relief to both parties. "Officer Banes, I know this lady, and I'll be responsible for her. Come back to my office, Mrs. Sterrett." She followed Buddy to his cubicle and sat down in front of his desk.

"Now tell me what this is all about."

Doris looked at him with a vacant stare. She spoke cautiously.

"I got pulled over for speeding. Sixty in a thirty-five-mile-per-hour zone or so says the goon out there in the blue suit. He asked to see my license and registration and was very rude and cocky, I might add. I couldn't find either and told him I was on my way home and if he would follow me, I'd show him when we got to the house. But he wouldn't hear of that. He made me turn off the engine and get in the car with him and come down here, and here we are. I told him who my husband was but that didn't faze him."

"Should it have?" Buddy felt some sympathy for the officer.

"Well, you seem to know me so I suppose you know who my husband is. Dr. Campbell Sterrett."

"Yes, I know you, and I know who your husband is, but, Mrs. Sterrett, that doesn't allow you to operate a moving vehicle without proper identification and a license."

Doris squinted at him and studied his face for a long twenty seconds and said, "Should I know who you are?"

"Lt. Buddy Briggs. I go to church with you every Sunday morning."

"I thought you looked familiar. I've seen you take

up collection. And your wife is Juanita, the real pretty auburn-haired woman who always sits over on the left side."

"Amanda."

"Yes. Amanda."

Doris made this revelation without the slightest bit of embarrassment. She saw no need to apologize in being slow to recognize him or remember his wife's name.

"Mrs. Sterrett, I think I can make this whole thing go away with Officer Banes out there …"

"Good."

"Let me finish. I can make it go away, run you home to get your permit, and smooth everything over with him. But what I can't do is release your car to you tonight."

"And just why not?"

"I have reason to believe if I insisted you take a test for alcohol consumption, you might have a little trouble passing. So why don't you just let me handle everything and let this whole thing die down quietly. We'll take you home and you can prove to Officer Banes you do indeed have a driver's license and then tomorrow morning you can pick up your car and drive it home."

Doris stood and waited for Buddy to lead her back to the front desk and make the arrangements. Then she went with Charlie Banes through the double front doors of the Mt. Jefferson Police Station and into the night toward certain agony and discomfort at arriving home in a city-owned police cruiser. That's what she *did*. What she *didn't* do was thank the lieutenant for his kindness or ever speak to him at church on any subsequent Sunday morning.

She hadn't acknowledged his existence until this very night, just a few hours earlier in her own living room. Now she had no choice. She would soon be his little girl's mother-in-law. She would soon be his grandchild's other grandmother. She would soon be the person they would have to plan their Thanksgiving dinners and Christmas mornings and birthday parties around. Would she be easy to work with? He wasn't expecting any miracles. As he sat watching the two sisters talk in low waiting-room tones, he became aware that one of them was raising the volume just a little.

Looking out the window toward the automatic door, Doris said, "Who called them?"

"Buddy called them. I felt like I needed him here."

Doris turned her cold bloodshot stare on Buddy, "Did you call them?"

Buddy finally realized whom she was talking about. Coming in the door and around the corner toward them were Paul and Dove Franklin. It was nearly one a.m. Their presence attested to the loyalty and care they showed to the members of their congregation. Colleen stood to greet them and they hugged and offered words of comfort.

A nurse came out and escorted the elderly woman, her daughter, and her son-in-law to one of the rooms at the end of the darkened hall. The young mother, who had walked the crying baby down to a coo and a whisper, was told they could come back, and the same nurse showed her where to go. This left the Milton Sandridge party of seven, which were engaged in intervals of sporadic conversation and awkward silence. At one low point of small talk, Dr. Sterrett came back into the room to an immediate hush in anticipation of news. He addressed Colleen, but spoke for all to hear.

"Milton has had a minor stroke. That sounds worse than it really is. There is no reason to believe he will not fully recover. It may take some time. A couple of months maybe, but he is going to be just fine."

"Oh, thank God." Colleen was visibly relieved. "Did you see him, Campbell?"

"Just for a second. Dr. Paxton is seeing to him. He's a good man. I offered to help in any way I could, although it's not really in my line. But he has everything under control, and I think you should be able to see him before long."

"Surely they're going to keep him."

"Oh, yes. He'll be here for at least a week I'd think. Maybe longer. But you just relax, and in about a half an hour, you'll be able to go back and see him."

"Thank you, Campbell. Thank you so much."

The conversation and the quiet roar picked back up and Buddy took this opportunity to call Amanda. Paul Franklin followed him out into the hallway.

"How did you find him, Buddy?"

"He was late coming home. Colleen called me so we went down to the store sometime after eleven and there he was slumped over his desk."

"I was with him today in that very office. I thought

he didn't look well. You're pretty close to him. What is it? The job? Does it demand a lot of him?"

Buddy had interrogated a lot of people but had not been interrogated himself since he was twelve years old when his daddy suspected him of smoking behind the garage. Is that what this was? An interrogation? Or was this just the thinning nerves at the end of one of the most trying days of his life? What did Paul suspect? What did he know?

"Probably the job. A lot of hours. And how about you? How's Millie?" When in doubt change the subject.

"Quiet. Very quiet. There's more to be done there. I'd like to talk to you about it after the holidays."

"Anytime."

"And by the way, you know I'm here for you where Shirley Ann is concerned. All you have to do is just call."

While Paul and Buddy talked in the hall, Doris turned her full attention to Dove, who was talking to Colleen about another parishioner who had suffered a minor stroke recently and recovered quickly and fully and was back stronger than ever at his job.

"What are you doing here?" Doris asked.

They both turned toward Doris.

"What are you doing here?" she asked again.

"Are you talking to me?" Dove asked.

"I'm talking to you. Your husband was called here tonight. But what are *you* doing here?"

"Doris!" Colleen said like a mother scolding a child.

"It's one o'clock in the morning. Do you always make hospital calls with your husband this time of night?"

"Sometimes I do. Yes, I most certainly do."

"When did that start? Our father is in this hospital. Have you ever been to see him?"

"I certainly have. I was here Monday."

"How about when our mother died? We were all at the hospital that night, too. Were you here? I don't think so."

"Doris, that was five years ago. I had a ten-year-old child then. I couldn't just leave anytime I wanted to. Now it's different. She's fifteen and can stay by herself. Is that what this is about? Because I wasn't here when your mother died?"

Colleen interceded. "Dove, that is not what this is about. Doris has had a very bad day and she's not herself. Please just ignore her and forgive her. She'll be better in the morning."

"Don't make excuses for me. I'm fine. And Miss Dove, if any other member of my family gets sick, don't feel obligated to come. Okay? But then you probably wouldn't anyway. You don't get out in middle of the night for just anyone, now, do you?"

Dr. Sterrett appeared mercifully behind Doris' chair. "Colleen, if you want, you can come back now."

He led her away, and the waiting room fell so silent you could hear the police calls coming in on Officer Tolley's radio. Someone had slipped in a ditch out on Route 250 but no one was hurt. A little shaken up, but nobody hurt.

CHAPTER

Walter was up and dressed by nine a.m. on Christmas Eve morning. He knew it was nine a.m. because as he was tying his oxfords, he heard the bells ring nine times from the steeple of the Mason Street Methodist Church. Dr. Yandall had already released him and made an appointment to see him in two days. Then he wished Walter a Merry Christmas.

Walter called Doris since he had agreed to spend the holidays at her house. He wasn't happy about this arrangement—he really would have preferred to spend it with Colleen and Milton, but then he did look forward to seeing Louis Wayne and Hoyt.

Doris and Colleen came in the room together and each kissed him on the cheek.

"Dad, are you ready to go?" Doris looked tired.

"I've been ready since five thirty this morning," he lied.

"Dad, there's something we need to tell you before we go."

He heard a seriousness in Colleen's voice that didn't match the season. Was it more news about his health? Certainly it couldn't get much worse than it already was.

"What's wrong now, sweetie?"

"We brought Milton in to the hospital last night. He's had a stroke."

Well, he was wrong. It could get worse.

She continued, "It was a minor stroke but he's going to be in here for a while. We found him at the store around midnight."

"Where is he now?"

"He's just down the hall. We can stop and see him on the way out if you want or if you don't—"

"Of course I want to." Walter picked up his small suitcase and started toward the door, but Doris stopped him.

"Dad, Campbell said you need to take a wheelchair down to the car. And let me carry that suitcase."

Walter turned and glared at her. "Let Campbell ride in the wheelchair. I can walk. Now what room is Milton in?"

"He's just down the hall," Colleen said, "in 226."

226. That had been Adrienne's room. Walter caught his breath.

The three of them walked down the hall and Colleen pushed the door open. Walter stood by the bed. Milton was sleeping, and Walter had been in this sanitized hell long enough to know not to wake a sleeping man. His eyes went from Milton's face to the walls, the ceiling, the floor, the windowsill. The building was old but then so was everything that held Walter's respect. Fifty years ago this room held little more than a bed and washstand. Now there were tubes and lights and buzzers and metal things that had no meaning to him whatsoever. Fifty years ago he was young and anxious and full of wonder. Now he was only anxious. He looked again at Milton, then turned and walked out. The women followed him.

"We'll take you home now." Colleen laid her hand gently on his back.

"No, honey, you stay here. This is where you belong. Doris can take me home. I'll be fine." He kissed her cheek and Doris took his arm and they walked past the nurses' station and waited in silence for the elevator.

When they were in Doris' 1958 Lincoln, he finally asked, "How's your boys?"

"They're fine, Daddy, but there's something I guess I need to tell you before we get home."

He looked at her out of the corner of his eye. Whenever she called him "Daddy" he knew something bad was going to follow.

"We have quite the situation at our house. Louis Wayne has been seeing a girl in secret—the Briggs girl. Shirley Ann. Do you know who I mean?"

He knew who she meant. He had seen them at church talking and giggling with one another, and if she hadn't been able to tell there was something in the air between those two, then she had been wearing blinders for eyeglasses.

"Well, we found out just yesterday she is expecting and believe it or not, it's Louis Wayne's. I know this is another shocker ... but I just want you to know what's going on in our house."

"Is Louis Wayne planning on doing the right thing by her?"

"Oh, yes. I'm afraid so. He's very determined."

"Determined, is he? Wonder where he gets that?"

"Is that all you're going to say about it?"

"What else can be said? He made his bed. He'll do all right. In my day people got married young. It didn't kill them. They survived. The boy has a lot of grit, Doris. Don't underestimate him."

Nothing more was said on the subject as they pulled out into the traffic.

"The drugstore is up here on the right. Do you need to stop for anything?"

Walter looked out the side window at the blue-cold day. The snow had stopped but the clouds remained. Icicles hung from the eaves of the buildings they passed. He didn't need anything from the drugstore but he did want to stop for something else.

"Nothing from the drugstore, but there is someplace I'd like to go before we go home. Drive through the cemetery. I want to stop at your mother's grave."

Without any question or comment, she did just that. She drove him in through the main gate, up the hill, and turned to the right and stopped the car by the Selman family plot. She came around and helped him out of the car, but then he said something she wasn't expecting.

"You stay here. I can make it okay. I want to walk up there by myself."

"Dad, you have no business—"

"I'll be okay. Just give me a few minutes."

Walter Selman walked alone through the cemetery reading tombstones as he went. First his father's, then his mother's, and then Ella's. *May they all rest in peace.* He stood for a moment at each while his daughter watched him from beside the car. Then he walked a bit farther and stopped at a small headstone near the stone wall. He stood there in the wind for a long time, and when he came back to the car, there were tears in his eyes. Doris said nothing.

As she drove the car back down the hill, she glanced over and noticed he had settled back in the seat and closed his eyes. Doris thought he was asleep, but he wasn't.

The community church choir continued to sing carols every night on the front lawn of the hospital and vowed to do so until Adrienne was well enough to be released. A few patients or their families complained about the noise, but for the most part, the quiet, respectful, and gentle gathering of well-wishers was well received. A hint of carnival joined the ranks when one of the downtown restaurants sent a wagon full of steaming coffee and the local bakery sent a cart of pastries and sold them to the freezing bystanders. But a reverent hush came over all when Lawrence Westerly, the hospital administrator, stepped out the front door onto the top step and made his announcement on Tuesday evening, the twentieth.

"Ladies and gentlemen. Mrs. Knoles is presently resting. She has had a very good day and is progressing better than the doctors had hoped for. I won't say she'll be out of here before Christmas, but she may be able to wave to you from her window. She thanks all of you for your support and your prayers and hopes that you continue exactly what you're doing. The doctors and staff send those same sentiments. The only thing I might add is to ask you to be careful about leaving any garbage on the lawn. Other than that, thank you very much for your support and have a good evening."

Before he could turn and walk back in the door, the choir began singing "Joy to the World" while the crowd offered cheers and applause for such good news. The news in the morning was even better. Mr. Westerly told them at ten o'clock sharp that Adrienne had had a good night, was resting easy, and sent her thanks to all who continued to pray for her. Walter was there for every announcement. He and his father still had their duties at the Crown, but he always took a break and ran up the street for the six o'clock news. The show at the Crown, which had been booked for months, was an unfortunate revue of a traveling chorale reading the history of a dozen famous Christmas carols and then performing them. Under ordinary circumstances this would have been a good-drawing show, but practically the same one was going on a block and a half up the street on the lawn of the local hospital for free and for a better cause.

On the morning of Thursday, December 22, 1904, Lawrence Westerly walked out the front door fifteen minutes late. The crowd had been mute since one minute after ten. The solemn look on his face telegraphed his words before he opened his mouth.

"Ladies and gentlemen of Mt. Jefferson, I do not have good news this morning. At precisely seven thirty a.m., Mrs. Knoles was rushed back into surgery due to a sudden infection. Dr. Larnette removed fourteen inches of her intestines. She is in a much-weakened state and little hope is being given her recovery. I am sorry to bring you this news." He went back inside, leaving the whole town in shock. Walter stood with the rest of the citizens, staring up at her window, longing hopelessly for her to appear there and wave.

"Walter." It was Dr. Larnette's unmistakable gravelly voice.

"Yes, sir."

"I'm going to my automobile. I'll be back in twenty minutes. When you see me, go to the back door the way you did before."

Walter's heart jumped. He knew that meant he would see Adrienne but he was nervous. He'd never seen a dying person before. He saw his grandmother just before she passed, but she had been asleep. And he had seen an uncle a week before he died, but he was sitting up dressed in his kitchen at the time. Before he let his mind wander too far into the uncertainty, his feet were propelling him up the hill toward Mason Street. He ran until he came to a large brick house on the corner. He jumped over the gate, ran to the door and knocked until a small sandy-haired man opened the door and smiled at him.

"Walter Selman. What are you doing out here on a cold day like this?"

"Mr. Blanchard, do you have any roses in your hothouse?"

"I wouldn't be surprised if I did. How many you need?"

"How many can you spare?"

Walter was standing at the kitchen door of Lenity General when Dr. Larnette motioned him inside. As they walked up the steps, the doctor looked over his shoulder and asked, "What's in the bag?"

"Flowers. That's okay isn't it?"

Larnette's unspoken approval stood firm as they continued toward room 226.

As before, he opened the door and let Walter in and then disappeared somewhere down the hall. The room was darker and smelled different than before. He walked to her bedside and heard her rustle the sheets.

"Walter. My dear, dear Walter. You have been so loyal."

Her hand glided up to his with surprising grace and she held it with a grip that contradicted her pallor. "You held me while I bled that night. You stayed with me when everyone else deserted me. You found Nick. I've been told you're never far away. And now look at you, you're here. And you've brought me something. What have you brought me?"

Too stunned and saddened to speak, Walter took four red, long stemmed roses out of the bag and placed them beside her on the bed. She touched them and smiled weakly.

"Four roses. So very, very sweet." Her voice was growing weaker with each word. "But why four, Walter? Why four?

"Matthew, Mark, Luke, and John,
The bed be blest that I lie on.
Four angels to my bed,
Four angels round my head
One to watch, and one to pray,
And two to bear my soul away.

"Do you know that poem dear, dear Walter? 'A Candle in the Dark?'"

"No."

She suddenly screamed loud enough to bring the doctors running, "Walter! I love roses."

And then she died.

CHAPTER

The morning before Christmas all was quiet in the Franklin household. Everyone slept late. Paul and Dove had been at the hospital until after 2 a.m. Millie thought ten o'clock was plenty early to get up on a non-school day simply because she was a teenager. But as peaceful as it seemed, a missing component spelled an underlying sadness. They missed the childish thrill of expectancy. The fact that tomorrow was Christmas should have brightened the household. But Millie wanted nothing this year and felt little passion about giving. There were no festive secrets. No last-minute surprises. No hidden gifts. No scheming. Christmas 1958 promised to be the least memorable of their collective lives.

Paul was in his study putting the final touches on his Christmas Eve sermon. He was reading, typing, reading, erasing, and reading again. He had been doing this for at least an hour and would have already been finished except for all the distractions that kept popping uncontrollably in his mind. He thought about the argument he and Dove had gotten into yesterday. The surprise walk together from downtown in the snow. His decision to look for a new church come January. Millie's brush with the law. Dove's insistence that she go to the hospital with him last night with the weather as bad as it was. And the final worry, the uncomfortable silence he felt when he walked into in the waiting room after talking to Buddy Briggs in the hallway. He had wanted to ask Dove about this on the way home, but it never seemed to be the right time.

Dove was in the kitchen making sugar cookies. It smelled like Christmas Eve even if it didn't feel like it. As he put the cover on his old Underwood, he considered all the ways he might get back that old Christmas feeling before the day was over. But first things first. He got up from his desk just as Millie was coming into the room.

"Daddy, what are you doing?"

"Working on tonight's sermon. I didn't know you were up."

"Daddy, can I say something to you?"

"Sure, sweetheart. You can say anything to me."

"I'm sorry about yesterday. I'll pay back all of those things out of my allowance. And in case you're worried, I promise I'm not going to do it again, ever."

"I'm glad to hear you say that on your own volition. But, sit down, honey, what I really want to hear from you is why you did it. What prompted you to take things that didn't belong to you?"

Tears welled up in her eyes and the willingness to talk she had brought into the room quickly faded.

"Don't get upset. You wanted to talk and that's what we're doing. We're talking. So talk to me. Tell me what was on your mind or in your heart."

There was a long pause. Paul waited patiently. If he failed her now, she might never talk to him again. She had made the entrée and he was just pushing the door open further.

"I wanted to hurt someone."

"Okay. Who did you want to hurt? Me?"

"Maybe."

"What if I told you I understand that? I understand

why you might want to hurt me. Maybe you want people to see you as more than just the 'preacher's kid.' That's fair, Millie. I have no problem with that. But, honey, you don't break the law to prove a point. Any point. Not God's law and not man's law. And if the point you wanted to—"

"That's not it."

"What?"

"That's not it. You're not who I wanted to hurt."

It was time for Paul to take a pause.

"I wanted to hurt Mr. Sandridge."

"Milton? Milton Sandridge?"

She merely nodded her head.

"Why? Has he ever done anything to you?"

"I wanted to steal things from his store and get him in trouble so he would be fired. That's not the first time I did it. I did it three other times and most of the stuff I just threw in the trash. Some things I kept, but I really didn't want them."

"You wanted him to get fired." This was more of a statement from Paul than a question. A statement to estab-lish firmly the new information he was still trying to digest. "Millie, why?"

"I don't know. I just don't like him."

"You don't like Mr. Zirk, your science teacher this year. Are you trying to get him fired too?"

"No."

"Then why Milton Sandridge?"

"Paul? Millie? Is there something wrong?" Dove was standing in the doorway with dustings of flour on her apron and her hands. "Have you heard something from the hospital?"

"No."

"It's just that I heard you mention Milton Sandridge. I thought maybe you had heard—"

"Who's in the hospital?" Millie asked, looking first at her mother, then her father.

"Mr. Sandridge. Your father and I were there last night. I left you a note on the bathroom door in case you got up and missed us."

There were plenty of currents in the air between family members, but none of them were connecting. Dove stood stillest of all, hoping her husband would pick up the conversation. Millie gave her attention to the edge-worn, room-sized rug in her father's study. And Paul, not focusing his eyes on any one thing, searched his mind over what had just happened. Aware that Millie had yet to tell him why she didn't like Milton Sandridge, he was even more interested in knowing if Dove had interrupted their conversation on purpose or if it was simply God's timing in forgoing an unpleasant situation. Millie was the first to speak.

"Are the cookies ready to be decorated?"

"They certainly are. That's why I came looking for you. Twenty-four Santas and twenty-four reindeer. Do you want to help, Paul?"

"No, I have to finish up in here. You girls go ahead. I'll be along in a bit."

He would talk to Millie later. He would talk to Dove later. Right now he would pray.

CHAPTER

27

Buddy, Amanda, and Shirley Ann were just finishing breakfast.

"What time did you get home last night, Daddy?"

"I don't know. It was late."

"I talked to Louis Wayne this morning. He said they hadn't heard anything yet today about his uncle. Do you think he's going to be all right?"

"I hope so."

"Well, I've got to get ready to go. Louis Wayne is picking me up shortly. His grandfather is coming home this morning and he wants me to see him. I really like Mr. Selman, don't you?"

"Yeah. He's a very nice man."

With one more gulp of juice and the slide of a chair,

Shirley Ann disappeared to ready herself for her future husband. Amanda looked over her shoulder at her still sleepy husband.

"You're talkative this morning."

"I just don't know what to say to her."

"It'll get better. This is only our second day. You haven't told me much about last night either. How bad was it?"

"Well, I saw first-hand the wrath of our new in-law, the stern Mrs. Sterrett. And on top of all of that, with Colleen on the verge of standing on her head, your good friend, the preacher's wife showed up."

"No!" Amanda turned from the sink and sat down in one of the dinette chairs.

"Yes. I was with the whole bunch till, oh, two o'clock I guess. Doris jumped Dove in the waiting room."

"What did she say?"

"She asked her what she was doing there right in front of Colleen."

"Oh, Buddy," Amanda put her hands to her mouth, "I feel like this is partly my fault. As a friend sometimes I just don't know what I'm supposed to do: let them cry on your shoulder or tell them the truth. What should I have done?"

"You did the right thing. It wasn't up to you anyway. But please, don't get any more involved in it than you already are."

"I promise you I won't. I'll just tell Dove we will have to talk about other things."

"Good. We've got plenty of our own worries without taking on their problems. Like our daughter. She's going from having a curfew to having a baby, just like that. She's going from having a bedtime to reading bedtime stories. We're in for a big roller-coaster ride, babe."

"I know."

"Where will they live? Has anyone thought about that?"

"She and I talked after you left last night. The Sterretts have a four-room apartment over their garage, behind their tennis court. She says it's very nice and cozy. All they'll need for now."

"So they'll be living with the Sterretts."

"No. Only close to the Sterretts."

Buddy laughed out loud. Amanda smiled and waited for him to let her in on the joke.

"Last night, sitting there looking at Doris, all I could think of was that drunk driving thing a few years back. Remember me telling you about that?"

"Now I do. I had forgotten all about that."

"Forgotten about it? How can you forget about things like that?"

"You need to forget things like that too, Lieutenant. You'd feel better if you did." And then she slapped him playfully on the shoulder with her dish towel as she got up and went back to the sink.

"Okay, I'll try to do better, Juanita."

They laughed, and it seemed a little more like Christmas Eve.

CHAPTER

28

"Now, Walter, you should have everything you need. You've slept in this guest room before. I'm going to the basement to get you a little television set with rabbit ears to put on that table."

His son-in-law was doing everything in his power to make him comfortable. His daughter was also flitting around the room, rolling back covers and fluffing pillows and taking lunch orders and basically making everyone nervous. Walter sat in the rocker and waited for them to wear down or leave. He just wanted to see his grandsons. They had gone to pick up Louis Wayne's girlfriend. Girlfriend? Or should that be fiancée? Future bride? Whatever her designation, he was content to sit in the old rocker and wait. It was a familiar chair—the same chair he had been rocked in as a baby, and Doris had been rocked in, and Louis Wayne and Hoyt had been rocked in. It was a comfort to relax in this old piece of family history. Old things brought peace and serenity to the most trying of times. And if he ever longed for the tranquility of heirlooms, he needed them today.

The room filled with doctors and nurses, and Walter was pushed so far from Adrienne's bed he could barely see her. Her eyes were open as if she were seeing a ghost, but Walter knew she saw nothing. Someone put a hand over her face, and when that hand was removed, she looked as if she had fallen asleep. Someone noted the time. Someone else scribbled frantically on a chart. The room was a blur of activity and noise. Dr. Larnette took him by the arm and led him to the hallway.

"Are you all right, son?"

"I'm not sure."

"Come sit down."

Larnette led him to a wooden straight-backed bench that had probably been used by friends and family members in very much the same condition of confusion and disbelief. The features of his face sternly set and his bald pate shining, the doctor sat down and spoke directly and quietly in his ear.

"Walter, the police will be coming up those stairs soon. If there is any last thing you promised that young woman you would do, you have to gather yourself up and do it now. You can still slip away unnoticed if you go soon. Is there someplace you have to go or something you have to do?"

"Yes, sir. I need to go find—"

"Don't tell me, Walter. Just go do it. Don't ever tell me. I can protect you better by knowing as little as possible. Now go."

Walter Selman walked briskly down the back steps, opened the door, and ran into the dark until his breath and heartbeat wouldn't allow him to run any longer. He didn't stop till he flopped down on the concrete steps behind the train depot. Here he caught his breath and his thoughts and began feeling his way down the lonely tracks leading north out of town.

When he thought he had come far enough, he stopped

and looked in all directions for the flickering fires. He saw nothing. Had he not come far enough? He walked a little farther and thought he saw one or two flickers over the embankment. He slid down the dirt bank, nearly falling more than once and continued slowly toward the dimly burning piles of brush and wood. When he looked around, he realized he was in the center of the camp. Or rather, of what *used* to be the camp. He smelled no food. Heard no voices. Saw no movement. The place was deserted.

"Nicholas! Nicholas! Nicholas Knoles!"

He walked to one of the fires and saw a broken plate and a tin cup and some rubbish lying in the dirt. He reached down to pick up a filthy blanket and a mud-caked glove.

"What do you want, boy?"

Too frightened to speak, Walter froze and backed away from the voice.

"I said what do you want?"

"I'm looking for someone who was camped here a few days ago."

"They're all gone."

"Where did they go?"

"Everywhere and nowhere." The voice took on a shadow as he moved closer and then took on human form as he came close enough for Walter to see his dirty clothes and the dried blood caked on the side of his face and melded into his hair. "The railroad jacks came and run everybody off. They do that every few days. You never know when they're coming with their billies and their cudgels."

"Do you know where Nicholas Knoles is? Was he run off?"

"Nobody uses names here, boy. Just one lost soul talking to another. He's probably thirty miles down the track. Which way, I can't say."

"Are you going to be all right? Do you need a doctor?"

"I don't need nothing. You wouldn't have any money on you, would you?"

Walter scrambled for the few cents he had in his pocket and dropped them into the crusty hand of the man who had no particular age and no particular place to go.

The man retreated into the shadows and Walter walked back up the hill, realizing he would never find Nicholas Knoles to tell him of his wife's death.

The town that had hoped and prayed for the hopeful recovery and then observed the quick demise of the young stage star turned out in overwhelming numbers to her funeral. Faith Presbyterian Church overflowed with every prominent family known to the local paper's social page. The mayor and his council sat on the front row. The doctors, who had worked without pay to see her through surgeries and a disappointing recuperation, filled the pews with their families. Merchants and farmers and out-of-town curiosity seekers stood around the walls and spilled into the subfreezing air on the sidewalk. A small theatrical orchestra made up of Civil War veterans played hymns and dirges from the choir loft. Three ministers officiated and spoke glorious words of praise over a life they had never known. Everyone attending the funeral service for this beautiful twenty-five-year-old actress was a stranger. E. G. Selman had tried to no avail to contact kin of any kind, even through the agency that had booked her into the Crown Theater. The police had telegraphed and telephoned her hometown. And Walter himself had tried to find her husband. It was the decision of the town fathers to bury her on Christmas Eve, so as not to dampen the spirit of the season by holding her body over until the following week. So at 2 p.m. on Saturday, December 24, 1904, Adrienne Knoles was eulogized in a house of the Lord and buried in a private plot in the Vestry Hills Cemetery.

Five men and one boy carried the casket up the hill from the horse-drawn hearse. The two black stallions stood in the cold, expelling steam from their nostrils while the tired soldiers marched behind, playing "Silent Night." Beautiful words of life and death were spoken, psalms were read. Only Walter saw the tall figure in a dark topcoat and slouch hat standing off in the distance by a maple tree. The man was sobbing.

At the closing of the grave, flowers covered the hillside, and that evening a light snow fell and covered the flowers. Adrienne Knoles was gone and so was Walter Selman's youth.

For years Walter scoured the entertainment papers. He found occasional mentions of Simon Croft, but he never made it back to Mt. Jefferson.

A legend grew as to the whereabouts of Nicholas Knoles. Townsfolk claimed to see a man walking the street at nights by the cemetery and swore it was the actor, come back to stand beside his beloved wife's grave. Sometimes it was reported a tall, strange figure would sneak into the old Crown and sit on the back row, only to leave before the show was over. And there were even reports that he had taken his life and that his spirit rested in the basement hallways of the Crown. But no one could give credence to such fiction, and eventually his mystery waned and went the way of all fables, myths, dreams, and memories.

CHAPTER

"Have Yourself a Merry Little Christmas" blended with a mother's and a daughter's cheerfulness that was long overdue in the Franklin household. Paul smiled to himself, wondering if perhaps some of his prayers were being answered. The phone rang and Dove hollered from the kitchen, "Paul, will you get that?" He did and after he hung up, he walked into the kitchen to see what all the merriment was about.

"You girls are sure making a lot of noise in here. Which one of you was singing with Gene Autry?"

"That would have been your daughter. She knows some of the silliest lyrics to 'Rudolph the Red-Nosed Reindeer' you have ever heard. She'll have to sing them for you sometime. How about you? Are you finished?"

"I think so. I'm not totally satisfied, but then I never am, am I?"

"Daddy, how do you write a sermon? I mean where do you get the ideas? From a book or something?"

"Yes, Millie. It's called the Bible."

"No, really, I mean do you buy sermon books or what?"

"Oh, you can. Outlines. That sort of thing. Some people use them more than others."

"How about you? Do you use them?"

"Very seldom."

"Then how do you know what to talk about?"

"Well," Paul looked thoughtful as he bit the head off a Santa Claus cookie, "I usually just talk about whatever is on my mind. Whatever I'm thinking about that week or worried about or suspect most of the congregation members are thinking about. If you just talk from your heart, you usually can't go wrong."

"What are you going to talk about tonight?"

"Christmas. What else?"

"Just tell the Christmas story? Wise men and shepherds and all?

It was clear to Paul that Dove was attentive to their

conversation. She smiled as she mixed up another batch of dough.

"No. Not necessarily. A little more than that you might say."

"What's the title?"

"'Forgiveness.'"

"Gee, that's kind of strange for a Christmas Eve sermon. I don't get it."

"I think it's perfect for a Christmas Eve sermon. It's where the story of ultimate forgiveness starts."

"Yeah, I guess you're right. I never thought of that. Mom, can I finish mixing those?"

"No, honey, I'm through. It's ready to be rolled out and then we can cut them."

Millie's attention was back on her father. She seemed to forget all about the cookies. Her eyes told him she had something else suddenly on her mind.

"Daddy, Mamma. You know what I'd like to do? You remember how we used to go downtown and eat lunch every Christmas Eve at Beecher's when I was little? Let's go today. We could walk down like we used to and eat hot dogs and ice cream sundaes. What do you say? Can we?"

Paul looked at his wife working dough with a rolling pin. He spoke to his daughter while never taking his eyes off his wife.

"I can't think of anything I'd rather do. You go wash the flour off your face and get your coat, and as soon as your mother, if it's okay with her, gets those cookies out of the oven, we'll head down to the big city and have a feast."

Millie left the room in a near run. Paul picked up the reindeer cookie cutter and began to make imprints in the flattened dough.

"Who was on the phone?"

"Colleen Sandridge."

Dove looked up in surprise. "Is everything all right?"

"Everything's fine. She was just calling to pass along an update. Milton is going to be all right. He'll miss Christmas this year, but he'll have a lot more ahead of him and she was thankful for that kind of good news."

"Paul." Dove began, then said nothing more until she finished placing the cutouts on the tray and shoving them in the oven. She wiped her hands on her apron. "Paul, you know I went to school with Milton back in Richmond."

"Yes, I knew that."

"And not just school. I went to the prom and football games and the Christmas dance and …"

"Yes, I knew that, too."

"Had I told you that?"

"No. Your mother did about ten years ago. One time when they were visiting, she saw him at church. That's when she told me."

"I'm sorry. I'm sorry it was my mother who told you and not me."

"So am I."

Paul went to the sink to wash his hands. Dove took off her apron and put it on the back of a chair. When she turned around, he was looking at her. She felt her face go flush and she dropped her eyes and began cleaning the countertop. When she looked up again, he was still watching, looking not just at her, but into her.

"Paul, from the first day I saw you on the stage at that Youth Council meeting at Radford, I have never been unfaithful to you. There have been moments … moments when I've been dishonest. But never unfaithful."

He had never demanded she tell him about affairs of the heart she had before they met, nor had she ever required the same of him. Her faithfulness as a wife and partner had never been in question. Not until this minute. Maybe the dishonesty she was confessing was of the spirit and not of the body. Did he want her to say it? Did he need to hear this from the woman he loved so dearly; the woman who was the mother of his only child; the woman who had been such an integral part of his life and mission. Her next words brought him back to the kitchen.

"Did you hear me? Dishonest. But never unfaithful."

"What does that mean, Dove ... dishonest?"

"I—"

"No ... wait. I don't want to know. This is all a bit difficult, Dove. I trust you. I believe you when you say you've never been unfaithful. But that dishonesty ... whatever it means ... it's still a broken trust, right?"

"Yes. And for that I'm sorry. So sorry."

Paul was silent for a moment, fighting the urge to pepper her with questions.

"Can you forgive me?"

Forgive her for what? Did he have to know the sin and all its detail before offering vindication? And just who would he be judging? Her or himself? She broke the silence again, showing a desperate need for his answer.

"Can you forgive me?"

He reached out and touched her hand and felt the same warmth he had felt the first time he'd held it so many years ago. He looked in her eyes and saw repentance for some unnamed sin. And he saw something else … something that had always been there, but somehow seemed truer in this moment. He saw her love for him.

"How could I not forgive you? That's what I do."

Just then Millie bounced into the room. She took her daddy by the arm and led him to the hall tree and held his overcoat while he put his arms in it and then socked an old hat on his head and they both laughed at how silly he looked. She yelled back the hallway.

"Come on, Mamma. Hurry up. We're ready."

Dove said from the kitchen, "Okay. I just need a minute."

CHAPTER

There was no knock on the guest room door to warn Walter someone was coming in. Hoyt burst into the room, high on Christmas, and jumped in his grandfather's lap.

"Well, hello, big boy. I sure have missed you." Walter hugged him long and hard, getting the same in return. Hoyt's big brother, Louis Wayne, was not far behind and he bent over the chair and unashamedly gave Walter the same hug. Standing back, in the doorway, was the prettiest and shiest blonde-haired girl Walter had seen since he was her age. The ponytail, the blue eyes, and the perfect smile asked in humble silence if she too should come in. Louis Wayne turned around and motioned to her.

"Granddad, this is Shirley Ann Briggs. You know

her from church and you've probably seen her at some of my ball games."

"I certainly do know her and once you've seen her at a ball game or a turkey shoot, you're not apt to forget her. And that, young lady," he said directly to Shirley Ann, "comes from an old codger who has seen a lot of pretty faces. But yours is one for the books. Come here and give me a hug."

And from that moment Shirley Ann was a part of the family. Walter had a way of putting his stamp on something and making it right for all who followed. Louis Wayne smiled big and sighed even bigger as Shirley Ann leaned over and pecked his grandfather on the cheek and then hugged him like they were blood kin.

They talked about Christmas and how cold it was. They didn't talk about Walter's illness. They talked about school and how much fun the next week of vacation was going to be. They didn't talk about Shirley Ann's pregnancy. They talked about gifts, and Walter asked Louis Wayne if he would go over to his house and pick up a few packages and asked Shirley Ann if she would do some last-minute wrapping for him, and she was thrilled that he would entrust her with such a task. Then they all listened to Hoyt tell about the cookies he was leaving for Santa and how last year he had actually heard reindeer hooves on the roof.

"I was going to see Santa this afternoon but now we're not," Hoyt said with a sudden sadness.

"Why's that?" Walter asked, though he already knew the answer.

"He was supposed to be at Uncle Milton's store, but something happened to his sleigh and he has to get it fixed so it'll be ready for tonight."

Walter listened as Louis Wayne and Shirley Ann added to Hoyt's Santa fantasies and then laughed with them as they related some of their own experiences with St. Nick through the years.

As the laughter died down, Walter spoke. "Shirley Ann, would you be so kind as to go down to Doris' sewing room, I think that's where she keeps the wrapping paper and bows, and gather up some ribbon and boxes and paper? Hoyt can show you where it is. Would you do that for me?"

"I'd be glad to, Mr. Selman."

"And then Hoyt can show you the tree and the train he has in his room. Take your time. I need to talk to Louis Wayne for a little bit."

The youngest and the newest members of the clan left the room hand-in-hand, full of Christmas secrets and plans, and Louis Wayne sat on the side of the bed and smiled proudly as he watched them go. His little brother and his fiancée were going to be the best of friends.

"Close the door, Louis Wayne, and come over here and sit down."

This is what Louis Wayne would miss most. His grandfather had never taken him fishing. He had never taken him for walks in the woods and shown him butterflies, and he had never taken him to a ballpark to see Mickey Mantle or Willie Mays. But he *had* spent lots of time with him eating ice cream cones and hamburgers and talking. They would ride around in Walter's Ford station wagon and talk for hours about things that mattered and things that didn't. One of his earliest memories was asking his granddad about the moon and why it was there some nights and not others. He asked him if God slept on the clouds and where people went when they died. He had asked him where babies come from and where the rain went. He asked him about girls and why they were different and why they made him feel funny. He was comfortable telling him who he got in a fight with and why, and his Granddad Walter always knew the right things to say to make him feel better. There was nothing taboo for the two of them and there never would be.

"How bad did your mother take the news about you and Shirley Ann?"

"Pretty bad. You told me weeks ago that I needed to tell her and Dad, and I know I shouldn't have put it off. But I really appreciate you not saying anything. If they had heard it from you it would have been a lot worse. I knew I had to be the one to tell them. I really think it's going to work out okay."

"What about her parents? The cop? I've always liked him. Did he want to wring your rotten little neck like I should have?"

"He's been great. I can tell he's biting his tongue, but so far so good."

"Well, good luck, boy. I don't know if I've always

done the right thing where you're concerned, but I've always tried."

"Granddad, you're the best. Always there when I needed you."

"Little pal, I need you now. I need you in a way I've never needed anyone else in my life. There is no one else on this earth that I trust or have the confidence in to understand what I'm about to tell you. But I want you to listen because what I'm going to say means a lot to me. Every word is true and not one word of it is meant for anyone else's ears but yours. Do you understand me?"

Walter began at the beginning. He began with the winter of 1904 and nine days before Christmas. He told Louis Wayne about the play, *The Nativity,* the Crown Theater, the husband and wife team of Nicholas and Adrienne Knoles. He left out nothing and nobody. He put all of his memories into words and painted as accurate a picture of the past as his sentimentality would allow. When he finished, he felt weaker and somehow transparent; as if he were made of glass, and Louis Wayne could see his bare, naked soul.

"I know where the grave is Granddad. It's close to where your parents are buried, isn't it?"

"It's in the family plot. My dad gave the lot to her because there was no other place to bury her. He put her clear over next to the wall, and, unless you know better, and only you do, you really can't tell it's in our plot."

"Does Mom know about this?"

"Nah. Everybody's dead that knew about it. Of course, everybody has heard a part of the story. The whole town knows about the mysterious grave in Vestry Hills and the woman with the traveling show who came through town around the turn of the century and got shot. You can look that up in the papers. They just don't know the story behind it."

"Why have you kept it such a big secret all these years?"

"Well, at first it was because of the police. They threatened for a long time to keep the case open and I was the only witness. There were even a couple of guys on the force who wanted to try to pin it on me."

"The murder?"

"Yeah. And then, as luck would have it, ole Bennington got caught up in a scandal and once the heat from all of that died down, the other had cooled off. I didn't want to perpetuate the legend because it always implicated me and shined suspicion on my family. Can you imagine what it would do to your mother if this whole story had gotten out? She would never show her face at the country club again if someone thought her old daddy had been tangled up with an actress and a murder years ago."

"I don't know what to say. Well ... I do have a few questions, though. Can I ask?"

"Fire away, little pal."

"Why *were* there four roses?"

"Cause that's all the money I had. If I'd had enough, there would have been four dozen. Old man Blanchard never gave a break to anybody. Good old fellow, but tight as a snakebite."

"Why did you tell me this today?"

"Well, you've heard the legend about it and how some mystery person puts flowers on the grave every Christmas but no one ever sees him? I know you've heard all those stories."

"I've heard about guys who have hidden behind tombstones on Christmas Eve to try and see who's leaving the roses. There was a story about it in the newspaper last year I think."

"There's a story about it nearly every year. But nobody is smart enough to catch that sly, mysterious, old man. You know why? Common sense. Sure, every year for over fifty years now there have been teenagers and college joes who have staked out the place and tried to see who was leaving the flowers. But you know it's cold around Christmas, and teenaged boys will sit out there for an hour and then lie and tell their friends they were out there all night, but it just isn't so. All you got to do is go out there at 3 a.m. on any Christmas morning and, believe me, there ain't nobody out but Santa."

Louis Wayne looked at his Granddad Walter's hairline; the white thick hair that still fell down across his forehead. He looked at his hands and saw an adventure in every wrinkle. He saw the creases above his eyes and the laugh that always seemed to dance around his mouth even when he was serious. He looked at his shoulders; still straight and strong enough to lift Hoyt over his head. But it was the emerald in the eyes that told him these were the same eyes that had seen it all so many, many years ago. The same eyes that had looked on Adrienne Knoles and held her secret and his for decades. Was he really the same age that Christmas as he himself was this very minute? Louis Wayne quickly did the math in his head and suddenly saw young Walter holding Adrienne in his arms in the basement of the old Crown. He saw him by the hobo camp looking for Nicholas. And he saw him sneaking in the back door of the hospital to bring her a final gift of flowers.

"Granddad, where do you find roses in the middle of winter?"

"Wherever you find love. Don't worry. You'll find them."

There was a long comfortable silence in the guest room as grandfather and grandson sat in contemplation of all that had been said. Each had their thoughts and, if truth be known, they were the same thoughts. They were the same blood. They were cut from the same cloth.

"Did you love her, Granddad?"

"Sure I did, little pal. Sure I did. And still do today."

CHAPTER

The skies were clear as the congregation began to arrive for the Christmas Eve candlelight service at the Mason Street Methodist Church. Falling snow would have made for a perfect scene, but the simple, bitter cold more than made up for the lack of precipitation. Women were dropped off at the front door while men parked cars in the lot behind the sanctuary or on the street by the curb. A rush of frigid air blew into the vestibule each time someone opened the front door. Splashes of color, red mufflers and green sweaters and Christmas corsages on coat lapels, filled the church, and the candles flickering in stained-glass windows sent a warm message to anyone passing by.

In every corner of Mt. Jefferson and in all the outlying areas, churches were duplicating the very same scene. Only the faces were different. Families left their dinner tables to worship and observe a simple service that would be the spiritual solace to a hectic season. There was no more shopping to be done. No more racing around town to buy last-minute ingredients for Christmas dinner or deliver last-minute gifts of cookies to friends. All that was left was Christmas.

You could see at least one other church from any one of the church parking lots. There were two Baptist churches, two Presbyterian, one Methodist, one Lutheran, a Brethren, and one Catholic church all within walking distance of one another. A bird's-eye view of the town would have made the perfect picture postcard.

Some came to church in casual clothes. Some in their Sunday best. Some brought neighbors who had never been. But they all came because they felt it was the right place to be. There would be enough evening after the service to put the little ones to bed and get ready for Santa's visit. Enough evening for families to get together and open packages with those they wouldn't see on Christmas Day. Enough time to slow down and take a deep breath and let all the tension out and allow a little of the peace in.

And that was what was about to happen at Mason

Street Methodist. The Rev. Paul Franklin was talking to choir members and watching the front door from his vantage point in a small room to the side of the pulpit. The seats were filling up nicely, and he was glad to see a lot of unfamiliar faces. He looked at his watch and wondered if Dove and Millie had left home yet.

Dr. Campbell Sterrett, Doris, and Hoyt came down the aisle and sat where they sat for every service: third pew from the front on the right. The organ was playing "Hark! The Herald Angels Sing" and Hoyt was playing with a yo-yo he had gotten as a gift from one of his school friends.

"I thought Louis Wayne and Shirley Ann would be here by now," Doris said leaning into her husband after they were seated.

"I'm sure they'll be along."

"Hoyt, put that thing in your pocket or I'll put it in mine. I told your father not to let you bring it."

Louis Wayne and Shirley Ann arrived and slid into the pew.

"Where have you two been?" Doris asked with a familiar scolding tone.

"We brought Granddad," Louis Wayne whispered.

"What? He's not here is he?"

"Yeah, he's back there talking to some people."

Doris turned her frustration toward her husband.

"Campbell, you know he has no business out on a night like this and in his condition."

"It's okay, Mom," Louis Wayne said. "He's feeling really good and he didn't want to sit at home by himself on Christmas Eve."

"Campbell, what are you going to do?" Doris asked. "Do you hear me? What are you going to do?"

Dr. Sterrett looked at the floor for a long time before finally raising his gaze to his wife. "I'm going to sit here, keep my mouth shut, and try to enjoy the fact that it's almost Christmas. And may I suggest that you, Doris, do the same."

Amanda stood just inside the two large, wooden doors that opened into the narthex. She smiled and spoke politely to other church members while waiting on Buddy, who was parking the car. She spotted Shirley Ann in the sanctuary just as Buddy walked up.

"Where do you want to sit?" he asked as he looped his coat onto a rack.

"Well, your daughter is sitting up front. Do you want to go up that far?"

"Who's she sitting with?"

"The Sterretts. There's room in the seat right behind them."

"I don't think so. I don't want to sit *behind* the Sterretts. That makes a statement I'm not ready to make."

"Oh, Buddy, don't be silly."

"No. Really. I mean it. There's room in front of them. Let's go up and sit in front of them."

"And that will put you practically on the front row, and I know you don't want to do that."

"Then what do you suggest? Just sit on the back row like we usually do?"

"No, I think we should sit with our daughter like we usually do. This may be the last Christmas we have that option and there's room in the same pew."

"So sit *with* the Sterrett family is what you're suggesting, Mrs. Briggs?"

"That I am, Lieutenant. You did leave your gun in the car, didn't you?"

"Why? Are you worried for me or for Doris?"

Paul still couldn't see if Dove and Millie had arrived. He had only a couple of minutes before starting the service and he always liked to see that they were seated before walking to the pulpit. It was just a little quirk he had developed over the years, like knocking on wood or touching the silver cross he wore in his lapel. He thought of it as a ritual, not a superstition. Such things couldn't take the place of religion, but they often did salve the insecurities of the human condition.

"Surprise, Daddy!" Millie poked him in the ribs from behind.

"Sorry we're late," Dove said as she folded her gloves and put one in each coat pocket. "We'll just go around and slip in the back." She leaned forward and kissed him on the cheek. It was a simple gesture but more meaningful to him tonight than it had been for years. Perhaps he had just found a new ritual to look forward to.

By the time Dove and Millie made their way to the back of the sanctuary, the choir had begun to sing "O Little Town of Bethlehem." Two of Millie's friends walked in and she turned to her mother and asked if she could sit with them.

"Sure." And they were off, leaving Dove standing in the open doorway. The church was full. Paul would be pleased with the turnout. Dove looked up and down the center and side aisles in search of an empty seat. She finally spotted one on the back row. As the choir began the second verse, she slipped in quietly and sat down. It wasn't until she reached for a hymnbook that she looked up to see who was next to her.

"Well, I wasn't expecting to see you here," Dove said.

"I wasn't expecting to come," Colleen answered. "But Milton was sleeping. I'll go back as soon as the service is over. I just needed to be here tonight."

There was magic in Paul Franklin's sermon. Everyone who heard his words felt the impact of them on their hearts.

Campbell Sterrett, sitting shoulder-to-shoulder with

his wife, heard a quiet tug on his spirit to soften his heart toward her. His son would be fine. Life would make Louis Wayne the man he was destined to be. Contending through it all with the woman beside him was where he needed more strength. This was his private prayer—to be granted the spiritual wherewithal to deal with his wife in her new role in their growing family.

Doris Sterrett looked down at her hands as Rev. Franklin's words rang in her ears. She knew she had to manage her emotions in a more acceptable way. She had to get a hold on herself and develop a healthy relationship with her daughter-in-law-to-be. Now was the time to drop her pride and admit the things that were most important. Isn't that what Paul said just a few second ago? "Forgiveness is first a private matter before you can pass it on."

Buddy Briggs knew better than anyone how difficult this sermon must be on Paul. He was pretty sure Paul thought the same thing about him. The boy sitting next to his daughter, not six feet away, was the core of it all for Buddy. He had to forgive him. He knew that. And he would. Maybe not tonight. Certainly not as easily as Amanda would. Amanda looked over and smiled at him.

He knew what was in her mind. She was seeing a newborn baby, a new creation, a new life that would make a difference in their family from this day on. She was incapable of *not* forgiving. That's just how her heart was built. He smiled back at her. He always did.

Millie Franklin was sitting with her friends, and Kay was passing a note back and forth between them. They did this often in church but tonight Millie wished they wouldn't. She wanted to listen to her father's words without distraction. They were touching her in a new way.

"There is love through blood that can't be denied or altered," he said.

She knew forgiveness was hers and she knew what she had to do with it. She closed her eyes there in the pew and made a promise never to knowingly do anything again in her life to hurt or humiliate her parents. And then she prayed for the will to keep that promise. When she opened her eyes, her dad was looking at her and smiling.

Louis Wayne and Shirley Ann wanted to hold hands but knew it would appear too pretentious in church … and next to their parents. Shared thoughts drifted between them. They both wanted to make everything right with their families. Shirley Ann wanted her dad to understand and her mother to know just how much she loved her for the support already given. Louis Wayne wanted his dad to say something—anything that would let him know how he truly felt. And he wanted his mother to let the world know a little less about how she felt. But all these wishes to be understood and accepted were overshadowed by the very real knowledge that *they,* the two of them, had put everyone in this awkward position. It was their actions that brought all these emotions to a head. The first and foremost need they felt, sitting there listening to Rev. Franklin, was God's forgiveness and a chance to make their lives matter. And that's what they silently vowed to one another with a quick glance as Paul Franklin said, "Forgiveness is always possible if first you have love." Just then Louis Wayne reached over and squeezed Shirley Ann's hand. Tears accented their eyes and they both felt a warmth of grace they would feel as a couple for decades to come.

Milton Sandridge was not asleep as Colleen had thought. He was staring at the ceiling of his hospital room and listening to the words of the Mason Street Methodist pastor over the radio. He knew the words were for him.

He felt the personal thump on his heart as Rev. Franklin said, "Struggling for the truth is hard but struggling *with* the truth is even harder." Milton didn't move. He just lay there waiting for the next word to fall, hoping in his heart that God would give him the mercy he didn't deserve.

Walter Selman sat alone on the back bench. He wanted to hear the sermon but also wanted to see the full scope of the people and the church. He and Ella often would sit in the back. How he missed her this night. She would have known just the right words to say to Doris and just the right blend of scolding and encouragement to offer Louis Wayne. And she would have made Shirley Ann feel welcome and still have found a graceful way to warn her about what she was getting into—about how to handle this side of the family. Yes, he missed her. He pretended for just a moment that she was sitting beside him until he couldn't stand to pretend anymore. Then he smiled a knowing smile and thought, *Isn't that what we do in life? We pretend until God shows us how.*

Paul had long disregarded his notes and was speaking from his heart. He, like the rest of the people in the sanctuary, was hearing these words for the first time.

He was talking to himself as surely as if he had been in his car alone rehearsing memory verses. All this talk of forgiveness was not advice for a captive audience; it was Paul working things out for himself. He thought of his daughter—a young lady reaching for independence and gaining the difficult wisdom of experience. He thought of his wife looking him in the eye and telling him she had been "dishonest" with him. As the day progressed and the Devil played with his suspicions, he became less and less certain about what she'd meant. But he was certain of one thing: God knew the difference. Paul's job was simple— to offer Dove the balm of forgiveness and accept love both coming and going. He spotted Dove and thought he could see tears in her eyes. Then he saw Dove lean over and put her arm around Colleen's shoulders.

"Colleen," she whispered, "It's going to be all right."

"Is it, Dove?"

"Yes. I promise."

Walter stood in the vestibule with the other deacons and handed out candy canes to kids and adults alike as they filed out at the end of the service. His family gathered at the front door and just then a soft sprinkle of snow began to fall. He said good night to Colleen and kissed her on the cheek and wished her Merry Christmas and watched as she went toward her car. Doris and Campbell stopped near the curb to wave good-bye to Colleen.

"Are you riding home with us, Dad?"

"No. You two go on ahead."

"How are you getting home?" his daughter asked.

"The same way I got here. Little pal and his girlfriend are going to take me."

Just then Louis Wayne pulled up in his car. Shirley Ann got out and climbed into the back, making the front passenger seat available to Walter.

Doris stood on the corner not believing this scene, but she laughed in spite of her mood at the sight of her father and son and his young fiancée piling into a car together.

"Well, just where are you three going and what time are you coming home?"

"Don't know," Walter said and he closed the door. "Could be pretty late."

Doris shook her head and smiled and waved and gave in to the spirit of the season. And as they drove away, they passed under a streetlight. Doris saw something lying in the back window. It looked like a bunch of roses. She shook her head. Where would anyone find roses on a cold winter night like this?

EPILOGUE

As I said at the beginning, I can see where almost all of it took place from where I'm sitting in my office overlooking Main Street. So much has changed and yet, with a little imagination, it's not difficult to picture it as it was. Macalbee's is now a local appliance center. The police station moved into a new building at the outskirts of town. Well, it's twenty years old now. The original building just up the hill from here is gone. In its place is a parking lot for the hair salon next door.

The Crown Theater, which had flourished for so long, died in the '70s when the new multiplex came in at the mall. It stood empty and dark for nearly two decades, but then a group of nostalgic citizens got together, raised some money, tore out the screen, and restored it to its original grandeur. Today it looks pretty much the way Adrienne Knoles must have seen it.

And the Mason Street Methodist Church? Still there. The congregation bought adjoining properties, tore down a few houses, and added a lot of Sunday school rooms and a fellowship hall, but all in all, it still looks the same as it did when the Franklins left the following year. They moved somewhere west; Illinois or Indiana, I think. I never really knew them but I did get to know Millie after she moved back to Mt. Jefferson. She taught high school here for years. She was my history teacher at MJHS. She was and still is a good friend to my parents, and, according to my dad and some old pictures I've seen, her mother, Dove, was every bit the beauty people said she was.

My great-grandpa Walter passed away quietly in his sleep—eleven years after that Christmas Eve—at the age of eighty-one. Turns out his illness was a virus just like they originally thought. For the undue agony he blamed the doctors, the doctors blamed the lab, and the lab blamed the technology. I didn't care who was to blame, I was just glad we had him all those extra years. I count that as one of my many blessings and I think he did too.

We spent many an after-school afternoon together just walking in the park, eating hamburgers and ice cream, and talking about anything and everything.

My great uncle Milton took an early retirement, and he and Aunt Colleen moved back to Richmond where he joined the family business. Office equipment I think. I never really knew them except for holiday get-togethers and a few family reunions.

Grandmother Doris and Pop Sterrett live in Florida and fish every morning and play bridge four times a week. She calls every Sunday night without fail and I have to tell her everything I had to eat for the past week, tell her what each of my kids did in school, and assure her that I'm still recycling. Pop seldom gets to talk but I know he cares.

Grandpa Buddy was offered the chief of police job, but turned it down and left the force. He took a less stressful job teaching a law enforcement class at a community college just down the road. And Grandma Amanda? Well, she held the family together. Some of the happiest moments in my life were spent in her kitchen and her backyard and simply in her presence. They, too, are gone and sorely missed. There's a picture of the two of them just over there on the bookcase. They were a handsome couple.

Uncle Hoyt is a doctor and lives in Europe. I'm not real sure where, as his address seems to change nearly as often as his marital status. My kids get birthday cards from him stuffed with money every year but no one has seen him since he stopped in to show off a new bride nearly ten years ago.

And Mom and Dad. What can I say? They didn't have it easy but they're still in love, and you can't get any better than that. Dad kept every promise he made at the precarious age of seventeen. He went to college, got his degree, and he and Mom raised three of us. We still get together on holidays and for family reunions. And though we enjoy Christmas mornings in our own homes, every Christmas Eve, we get together at Mom and Dad's for an old fashioned bow-and-paper-strewn living room Christmas celebration with kids rolling on the floor and more food than ten families could eat. For some of us it's a shorter night than it is for others. But no matter what time I finally get to bed, I can always be assured that sometime around 3 a.m., Dad will be sitting in the car in front of the house with two cups of coffee, waiting for me. To most people a middle-of-the-night Christmas Eve adventure might seem an imposition at best, or a fool's errand at worst, but we wouldn't miss it for all the roses in the world. Or even just for the eight long-stemmed ones that are always lying on the backseat of his car.

Four for Adrienne. And four for Walter.

... a little more ...

When a delightful concert comes to an end,

the orchestra might offer an encore.

When a fine meal comes to an end,

it's always nice to savor a bit of dessert.

When a great story comes to an end,

we think you may want to linger.

And so, we offer ...

AfterWords—just a little something more after you

have finished a David C. Cook novel.

We invite you to stay awhile in the story.

Thanks for reading!

Turn the page for ...

- **A Conversation with Don Reid**
  - **Discussion Questions**

A Conversation with Don Reid

What was the original inspiration for *O Little Town*?

Around the turn of the century, a member of a traveling circus troupe was murdered in Staunton, Virginia, the town upon which this story is based (and also my hometown). Her name was Eva Clark. Every year mysterious flowers are placed on her grave. That was the inspiration. The rest is fiction.

What sort of research did you do as you wrote this novel?

I love research books. I have loads of them. I used them to check dates and become familiar with fashions and learn about common expressions from the early 1900s. I didn't have to do much research for the 1958 storyline—I just referred to my own memories. I was only a kid then, but I was deep into that decade with my formative years.

Which character (or characters) do you relate to most in the story?

This may sound corny, but there's a little bit of me in each of the characters. In order to really know them and develop them, I think I had to become a part of their thinking process. I love Walter—his grumpiness and wisdom. His matter-of-fact look at life. And I found Dove attractive even though she was full of problems of the heart. I really liked all these people. Even Doris. (Every family has one.)

How did you approach the writing of this novel? Did you map out the story before you dug into the writing, did you follow an idea to see where it took you, some combination of the two?

I did my own strange outline. This wasn't anything like I learned in creative writing classes in school. I listed all my characters on a legal pad and drew lines from one name to the other and then wrote on the lines what their

after
words

relationship was. Then I made notes about what I wanted to cover in each of the chapters—just three or four lines to remind me where the story would go. I knew from day one how the last page would read.

As the book took shape, what surprised you most about the characters or storyline?

I don't think anything about the storyline surprised me, but the people did. They all were more complex than I first thought—less "black and white." There were no goodie-goodies and not a devil among them. They were the people next door and I was just looking in their windows.

How would you describe the role of faith in *O Little Town*? The role of family?

The whole punch to the book is forgiveness. Every character whose family played a role came from a strong and good and faithful family. Some of the folks in the 1904 storyline didn't have strong family connections. They were just out there drifting. And without God we all would be.

What was the most rewarding aspect of writing *O Little Town*? The most challenging?

The most rewarding thing was seeing these people leap from my mind to the paper and take on life. That, and having people respond with a smile after reading it.

And the most challenging? Keeping the timelines in order. Making sure the ages checked out and worked within the time frame.

What do you hope readers will take away from the story?

I hope they're entertained, inspired, and moved. I hope they recognize in the characters people in their own lives, and perhaps even see themselves in there somewhere.

DISCUSSION QUESTIONS

Gather some friends together after reading *O Little Town* to talk about the themes and characters. Use these questions to spark a lively discussion.

1. What's your initial reaction to the main characters in the story? What did you like about them? What did you dislike?

2. What intrigued you most about the storyline that was based in 1904?

3. In what ways were the two different time periods similar? What were the most striking differences?

4. What did you learn about Walter from the way he reminisced? From the way he interacted with his family?

5. What surprised you most about Adrienne? About young Walter?

6. What were some of the main characters' greatest areas of personal growth?

7. Which storyline was most compelling to you? Which one could you relate to most from your own experience?

8. Which character do you relate to most? Why?

9. What role did the Crown Theater play in the story? Macalbees? What are some of the buildings or locations that play important roles in your life?

10. Describe your first impression of Millie. How did those first impressions change over the course of the novel?

11. What role does forgiveness play in the two storylines?

12. What does the novel teach about the role of families?

13. What role does faith play in the lives of the main characters? In what ways do faith and family intersect?

14. What story element made you most uncomfortable? What made you want to stand up and cheer?

15. Describe acts of heroism and acts of cowardice from the story.

16. What kind of sacrifices did the main characters have to make in this story? What does that tell you about their character?

17. In what ways did this story inspire you? Challenge you?

18. How did the imperfections of the characters play into the story? In what ways did they seem "real" to you?